ARBITRARY AND CAPRICIOUS

Jim Lively

TREATY OAK PUBLISHERS

Publisher's Note

**Printed and published in
the United States of America**

Treaty Oak Publishers

ISBN 978-1-959127-03-1

also by Jim Lively

ABERRANT BEHAVIOR
CHOKING ON THE SPLINTERS
PUNITIVE DAMAGES
THE PUZZLE AESTHETIC
SURREAL ABSURDITY

Available on Amazon

DEDICATION

This novel was influenced in part by my experiences as a corporate attorney for many years. It is dedicated to all the friends that I was fortunate to have made at Electronic Data Systems Corporation.

Chapter 1

"Sanders, care to check out the gallery?"

"Yes, let me just finish this email and I'll be right with you." Sanders exited his office and rounded the corner to enter the main gallery space.

Taylor stood on a ladder, adjusting a light directed down at a painting on the south wall. He walked over and stood next to the ladder.

"The lighting looks nice on that piece."

Taylor flashed a smile. "Would it be better if I directed this other light on the painting?"

Sanders rubbed his head. "No, I think it looks fine." He glanced at his watch. "Let's get a glass of wine and then we can check out all the lighting."

She climbed down from the ladder. "I know your rule about the need to enjoy wine while viewing art."

Taylor Miller, a talented, beautiful, upper twenties woman, was a brunette, with lovely pale skin and piercing mahogany brown eyes. Sanders had first met her when she attended the grand opening of his art gallery, Interurban Contemporary, located in the Core District of Richardson, Texas. She gave Sanders' a card with her website, and he promised to check out her work.

Several months later, while searching for something in his desk drawer, he came across her card. Sanders agreed to exhibit Taylor's work at an exhibition in his gallery. They had developed a friendship which culminated in Taylor working part-time for him while she searched for a permanent position elsewhere.

Sanders opened the small refrigerator behind the bar and pulled out a bottle of Markham Chardonnay. He poured two glasses and slid one across the bar to Taylor. "How's the job search coming?"

She moaned. "Tedious. The right type of position is just not available. I'm getting very frustrated."

He leaned forward on to the top of the bar. "Sometimes, you just have to be patient. Take me, for instance. I practiced law for all those years before I discovered that all I really wanted to do is paint and run an art gallery."

"Sanders, I really appreciate your letting me help around here. I know you could manage the gallery fine without my help."

Sanders gestured toward the ladder. "I'm getting too old to be climbing around on a ladder, tinkering with the lighting. I really appreciate your doing that and your good eye for curating. Your fine art education is certainly reflected not only in your art but also in your view for what goes where in an exhibition."

Taylor smiled. "Thank you. I just hope I can get a job soon with some museum or college."

Sanders' phone rang from inside his office. "It's

probably a salesman or something but I better go see who's calling."

He hurried off to his office and answered on the fourth ring. "Hello."

"Is this Charles Sanders Pierce?"

Sanders wrinkled his forehead. "Yes."

"The Charles Sanders Pierce who left the practice of law to become a famous artist?"

Sanders laughed. "Yes, to the first part about leaving the practice of law anyway. Who's this?"

Giggling came from the other end of the line. "This is your former colleague. Don't you recognize my voice?"

"Jackie? How in the world are you doing?"

"I'm doing fine, Charles. Oh, excuse me, I heard you go by Sanders these days. How are you?"

Sanders leaned back in his chair. "I'm doing fine as well. Are you still General Counsel for Global Data Systems?"

"Yes, going on a year now."

"Are you interested in purchasing some art or are you calling just to reminisce?"

She sighed. "I wish I were just calling to reminisce, but I'm actually calling to ask a favor."

Sanders picked up a pen resting on his desk. "Really?"

"Yes, Sanders. Would you consider a temporary contract job with Global Data Systems?"

"Jackie, you're aware I haven't practiced law in over five years now? I cannot fathom what value I could possibly offer."

"In a word, Sanders, integrity. I need someone void of any conflict of interest to help with a corporate internal investigation of sorts. You used to be an expert in health benefits. That's a critical part of the investigation."

Sanders doodled with his pen on a legal pad of paper. "The operative words there are 'used to be'. A ton of changes in the federal law governing health benefits have come down the pike in the five years since I retired. Surely you must have some attorneys in your department who could handle this matter."

"Yes, but that's where the conflict comes into play. They're employees of Global Data Systems. The government would not perceive that as an independent investigation."

Sanders inhaled and held his breath for a moment. "Couldn't you hire an outside law firm to handle this instead?"

"I've tried. Every major firm I've contacted either has a connection with Global Data Systems, or one of its client companies, or worse yet, one of its competitors. Global Data Systems has two major competitors that provide the type of data processing and health benefit claims administration to large corporations across the United States."

"Jackie, I've represented a lot of insurance companies over the years. It's possible I have a conflict of interest as well."

Jackie chuckled. "Don't you think I thought of

that? I still have some pull at our old law firm. They ran a 'conflicts check' of all your old clients. It came out clean."

Sander rubbed his forehead. "Couldn't you just hire the attorney who replaced me when I left the firm?"

"Impossible. You're referring to Barbara Strom. She has a conflict as well. Barbara used to practice in-house with IBM. As you may suspect, IBM is a major competitor of Global Data Systems."

Sanders ran his hand over his bald head. "I'm not sure, Jackie. I'm really enjoying not practicing law."

"I understand, Sanders. However, would you at least come in and discuss the matter with me?"

He sighed. "I'm very hesitant. How long would this job take anyway?"

"A month or maybe two at the most. If you will meet with me, I'll even buy you lunch in the company cafeteria."

"I thought you wanted me to show up." Sanders tsked-tsked and then paused. "I tell you what. If you delete the lunch in the cafeteria proposal, I'll agree to come in and visit with you."

Jackie laughed. "Corporate cafeteria food isn't too enticing, is it?"

Sanders snorted. "Not unless you happen to have a taste for prison food."

"Okay, Sanders, you win. Are you free next Tuesday at 2:00 p.m.?"

"Just a moment, let me check." Sanders accessed

the calendar on his phone. "Wide open."

"Fantastic. My secretary will have you cleared with security at the gate."

Sanders scribbled the date and time on a legal pad. "I'll see you next Tuesday, but please don't expect me to say 'yes' to whatever it is you want me to do."

"No problem. I'll see you Tuesday. Bye, Sanders."

Jackie hung up before Sanders could respond. He stared down at the legal pad.

Why did I agree to even discuss the matter with her?

Sanders rose from his desk and ambled out of his office and back into the gallery. Taylor was sitting at the bar, staring down at her cellphone, which lay next to her empty wine glass on top of the bar.

He spotted her empty glass. "Care for a refill?"

She glanced over at his full glass. "No, I'll wait for you to finish your glass first."

He chuckled. "After that phone call, I may down it in one gulp."

Taylor wrinkled her forehead. "Did you get some bad news?"

Before answering, Sanders walked behind the bar and picked up his glass. "That was a former colleague of mine." He paused to take a swig of wine. "She's general counsel with a large corporation and wants to retain me on some temporary work assignment."

Her eyes widened. "Really? Are you going to do it?"

Sanders sighed. "I agreed only to meet with her

and visit about the matter. I cannot imagine taking up any type of legal work now. I'm content with being an artist and running a gallery."

Taylor smiled. "If you do decide to take the job, I'm more than happy to cover for you here."

He finished off his glass of wine. "Thank you. I appreciate the offer. Let me pour us both a refill and let's go discuss art."

* * *

Sanders drove the short commute home from the gallery that evening. He had surrendered the view he enjoyed in his downtown apartment for a townhouse he purchased a few months earlier in Richardson. Sanders chose it because it was only five miles from his gallery.

As he waited for the front gate of his community to open, he pondered what kind of job Jackie would ask him to do for Global Data Systems. Then he all but made up his mind to turn her down.

Chapter 2

S anders glanced up at the wall clock in his living room. It was 1:00 p.m. He had just enough time to change clothes and make the trek up north to the Global Data Systems sprawling campus on Legacy Drive in Plano. Sanders climbed the stairs to the third floor of his townhouse and entered his bedroom.

He had taken care to select a pair of gray slacks and light blue dress shirt, reminiscent of his previous career, which he laid out on top of his bed. Fast as he could, he changed his clothes and slipped on a pair of black runners with white soles. Sanders smiled at the thought of wearing runners to a corporate meeting. That would never have crossed his mind years earlier when he was practicing law. Back then, it was strictly white dress shirt, conservative tie, charcoal gray suit and freshly polished black dress shoes. He grabbed a navy sport coat out of his entry hall closet before exiting his townhouse.

After maneuvering through light traffic while driving north on the North Dallas Tollway, Sanders eased his FIAT Spider up to security guard's station and shifted it into park as he waited for the guard to approach his car. The guard check his credentials, handed him a plastic Visitor Badge, and opened the gate.

Sanders slipped the badge into his coat pocket and followed the directions to park in Visitor Parking, located about thirty yards from the front glass doors. Walking through the parking lot toward the doors, a shiny black Porsche 911 passed him first, trailed by a red Jaguar F-TYPE. Both cars disappeared into a small underground parking garage near the front door. Sanders surmised that this parking garage was reserved for corporate VIPs.

He entered the building and right away a security guard asked to see his Visitor Badge. Sanders fished the badge out of his pocket and handed it to the security guard.

As the guard snapped it onto the front pocket of Sanders' sport coat, he growled, "Make sure your badge is visible at all times while you're on campus."

Sanders nodded but did not reply. The guard pointed in the direction of a huge reception desk. As he made his way over to the desk, Sanders surveyed the lobby. The carpet was an industrial gray tone prevalent in modern office buildings built since the late 1990s.

A large bronze sculpture of an eagle perched on a pedestal stood in the middle of the lobby. Sanders would later learn that the eagle was Global Data Systems' corporate symbol. The artwork adorning the walls was minimal and seemed to have been selected to blend in with the gray and navy blue furniture.

When he approached the reception desk, a young twenty-something blonde, dressed in an impeccable white shirt and gray pantsuit, looked up from the desk and flashed a smile. "Good afternoon, Mr. Pierce."

Sanders eyes widened. "Good afternoon. I can see you're very efficient."

"Ms. Vanderweel is on her way down to escort you to Legal Affairs." The woman pointed toward her left. "Please have a seat over there"

Sanders nodded. "Thank you. Will do."

Five minutes passed before an elevator across the lobby opened and a thirty-something brunette woman exited. Sanders watched as she made a beeline across the lobby in his direction, trying not to yawn at her boring corporate wardrobe choice, a navy blue pantsuit and light blue shirt. When she was within a few feet, Sanders rose from his seat.

She said, "Mr. Pierce?"

Pierce smiled. "Yes."

"I'm Beverly Vanderweel, Ms. Rogers' administrative assistant."

"Pleased to meet you, Beverly."

Beverly gestured with her left hand. "Please follow me."

The two did not speak as they rode the elevator up to the tenth floor. When the doors opened, Sanders noticed that the carpet was much plusher than the lobby. The furniture was all matching dark leather and the artwork on the wall featured engaging abstract landscapes. Sanders wanted to inquire about the artist but chose to remain silent.

He followed Beverly down a long hallway to a closed door with the words 'Legal Affairs General Counsel Conference Room' imprinted on a brass plate. Beverly opened the door. The small conference room offered a stunning view of the Global Data Systems campus ten stories below. Around a maple conference table, eight dark leather chairs had been positioned, spaced evenly apart, with specific care.

"Please have a seat," Beverly said. "Ms. Rogers will be with you soon."

Five minutes later the door swung open, and in floated the familiar voice of Jackie Rogers giving some last-minute instructions to Beverly. "Tell Bryan to give me a call this afternoon to update me on the Sterling matter."

Jackie was frowning when she entered the room and closed the door behind her with her left hand. She clutched a file and legal pad in her other hand. Her face lit up when she made eye contact with Sanders. She rushed around the table and gave him a quick hug.

"Putting out some last-minute fires?" Sanders said with a smirk.

Jackie rolled her eyes. "You couldn't even imagine." She gestured for him to take a seat. "Thank you for coming in to meet with me."

Sanders sat back down in his chair. "You're welcome."

She crossed the room so she could face him and sat down. "Before we get started. How have you been?"

He leaned back in his chair. "I'm doing fine. Just leading a quiet life and enjoying being an artist."

Jackie sighed. "I'm envious. Maybe someday I can retire."

"How's being General Counsel of Global Data Systems working out for you?"

She wrinkled her forehead. "It can be challenging at times. I deal with a lot of different problems, more than I dealt with in private practice."

Sanders nodded. "I'm sure that's right."

Jackie opened the file folder and slid the contents across the table to Sanders. "I hate to ask you, but I need you to sign a non-disclosure agreement. Are you okay with that?"

Sanders' eyebrows shot up. "You want me to sign an NDA just to tell me about whatever it is you want to discuss with me?"

She pursed her lips. "I trust you implicitly. But this is a very delicate issue. This is standard procedure for anyone doing sensitive contract work."

Sanders picked up the two-page agreement. "Give me a second to read it."

Jackie leaned back in her chair. "Take your time. I assure you that it's very standard."

Sanders spent less than two minutes to peruse the document. After signing it, he scooted the folder across the table to Jackie. "Okay, what's next?"

She forced a smile. "Thank you. Now let me give

you some specifics. As you may know, Global Data Systems handles the data processing and claims adjudication for health benefit plans for hundreds of large corporations across the United States. This is sensitive personal health information. Clients entrust us to perform these operations with the upmost in discretion and privacy. In some—"

Sanders cleared his throat. "Not only that, but it's also federal law."

Jackie groaned. "Yes. May I please continue?"

He sighed. "Of course."

"Our contracts attempt to limit Global Data Systems' exposure to the extent possible. But as you know, the court cases are trending toward finding us and our competitors as fiduciaries when we perform claims adjudication, regardless of what the agreements state."

Sanders leaned back in his chair. "That holds you to a higher standard of review and makes you potentially more liable for any mistakes."

She nodded. "Precisely. We're aware of at least two cases from the Beta Account where someone or something has leaked sensitive health information. In one case, it involved a diagnosis of AIDS. This individual notified his corporate security, complaining that some stranger contacted him about his medical condition. The other company's security alerted our head of Corporate Security, who had the matter investigated."

Sanders tapped his pen on the legal pad in front

of him. "Did Corporate Security uncover anything?"

Jackie shook her head. "No, not a thing."

"You mentioned there was a second case."

"Yes, the second case was with another corporation. It also involved the leak of medical information concerning an employee's treatment for a sexually transmitted disease. This guy received an email concerning his disease from an unknown source."

Sanders leaned back in his chair. "Couldn't the culprit be someone outside of Global Data Systems who got hold of the medical information?"

Jackie ran her hand through her hair. "Yes, it's possible but not likely. In both cases, the emails contained a Global Data Systems Explanation of Benefit form. As you know, when a claim is decided on its merits, the participant in the health benefit plan is given an EOB informing him or her of the decision made on the claim. In both these cases, each one received an email containing a fake EOB before he or she had received the actual one through proper channels.

Sanders grimaced. "Talk about arbitrary and capricious."

Jackie wrinkled her forehead. "What?"

"That's the standard of law in this area. If a fiduciary's action under its health plan is deemed by the court to be arbitrary and capricious, the court will rule for the plaintiff who is suing the plan. I'm sorry to digress. How long ago did all this occur?"

"A couple weeks ago."

"As far as you know, did either person receive a second email?"

She frowned. "No, we're not aware of any. I don't know if this is one of our employee's idea of a prank or if something more nefarious is involved. Regardless, these types of occurrences will destroy Global Data Systems' integrity. The loss of even a dozen large agreements would tank Global Data Systems' stock. Of course, there's the financial exposure from various lawsuits. Finally, if the matter hasn't already, it will get the attention of the federal government. First, the Department of Labor will conduct an audit, followed by the SEC and IRS. You can imagine the headaches that will cause."

Sanders scratched his head. "So, where do I fit in all this?"

Jackie leaned forward and rested her elbows on the conference table. "I want you to perform a thorough due diligence investigation of the account that is involved so far and any others that might emerge."

"What makes you think I can uncover something your own Corporate Security could not expose?"

Jackie's eyes widened. "You're a seasoned attorney who specialized in health benefits law. As I recall from our time together in private practice, you can be quite tenacious and meticulous in your investigations. You will be given a private office, private telephone line, and a confidential email address."

Sanders leaned back in his chair. "What incentive will employees have to cooperate with me? I don't want to be sitting in my office surfing the internet."

"They will have plenty of incentive. As a condition of employment, every employee must sign an agreement to fully cooperate in any matter involving our clients. That agreement contains thorough non-disclosure provisions about any aspect of their employment related to the performance of activities on behalf of our clients. Employees at a higher senior level are required to sign even more stringent agreements. I suspect the rumor mill has already started internally about the illegal information disclosed in these two accounts. Employees know they will be held accountable for any breach of their responsibilities to the maximum allowed under civil and criminal law."

Sanders eyes narrowed. "Have you considered offering an additional incentive for employees to step forward with helpful information?"

"You mean like a bonus if an employee provides useful information?"

He nodded. "Precisely. If the information leads to the identification of the culprit or culprits."

Jackie made a note on her legal pad. "I'll have one of my labor attorneys research that."

"If I agree to accept this contract job, I'll need a lot of information in advance so I can adequately prepare and hit the ground running."

Jackie smiled. "But of course. I have already assembled a detailed organizational chart for the account where an improper disclosure of information occurred and a flow chart overview of each step along the way when a health claim is processed and adjudicated. What else would you like to see?"

Sanders looked up from writing on his legal pad. "Off the top of my head, I would want to review the employee contracts for all levels of employees and the agreements Global Data Systems have with the clients impacted by the breach."

Jackie jotted down some notes on a legal pad. "Anything else?"

He said, "What kind of compensation are we talking here?"

She pulled an envelope from another file and slid it across the table to Sanders. "This is the offer."

Sanders opened the envelope and removed the contents. He perused the three pages. His eyes widened and he glance up at Jackie. "Is this amount correct for a month or two of work?"

Jackie nodded. "Yes, getting to the bottom of this matter is a high priority for the corporation.

He leaned back in his chair. "A hundred thousand dollars is a lot of money, regardless of the high corporate priority."

She said, "Any other questions?"

He shook his head. "No, I just need to decide if I want to tackle this project. If I turn it down, it won't be because I was dissatisfied with the compensation."

She set her pen down. "I know you need some interval to decide but time is of the essence. I would not be surprised if we're informed of another breach soon. God knows how many times the affected individual chose to remain silent rather than reveal that his or her health information was improperly disclosed."

Jackie glanced at the clock on the wall. "I have another meeting in ten minutes. All I ask is for you to give this matter careful consideration. It would definitely help me out."

Sanders inserted the offer back into the envelope and slipped it into his coat pocket. "I promise I won't take long in deciding."

She stood up. "Thank you, Sanders. I'll have Beverly escort you down to reception."

* * *

While driving south on the North Dallas Tollway, Sanders kept mulling over the meeting with Jackie.

I feel so conflicted! A hundred grand would pay all the expenses of the gallery for several years!

On the other hand, I want to help an old colleague, but I'm so hesitant to get involved in a corporate quagmire of problems!

Chapter 3

After his meeting with Jackie, Sanders headed back home instead of going to his gallery. As he approached his townhouse, a woman clad in black yoga pants with pitch black hair opened the mailbox in front of the townhouse. Sanders had not seen or met her before. He wondered who lived in the next-door unit. He drove up and stopped his car behind her and rolled down his window.

The woman whipped her head around. Sanders judged her to be in her late forties. She had pale skin and wore very dark eye makeup. To Sanders she resembled Siouxsie Sioux, of the old punk rock band, Siouxsie and the Banshees.

The woman barked, "Were you my 3:30 p.m. appointment? If so, you're five minutes late!"

Sanders wrinkled his forehead. "No, but I believe, though, I'm your next-door neighbor." He gestured with his head at his townhouse. "I live there."

The woman's face softened. "Oh, sorry."

He smiled. "No problem. I'm Sanders."

She took a step forward and extended her hand. "I'm Claire."

They shook hands. Sanders could not help but notice she had a strong and forceful grip.

"I take it," he said, "someone missed an appointment with you."

Claire groaned. "Yes, some of these guys are real flakes."

Sanders narrowed his eyes. "May I ask, what do you do?"

Claire stared at him a few seconds before answering. "Let's just say I provide a type of psychotherapy in a non-traditional sense. A power exchange type of thing."

Sanders rubbed his head. "I'm not sure I understand."

Claire smiled. "If you ever needed my therapy, you would understand. Listen, I have to run."

"Okay, Claire. It was nice to meet you."

Claire waved at him, acknowledging his comment, but did not say anything else. Sanders shifted the Spider into drive and eased into his driveway.

I certainly can't say I have the friendliest of next-door neighbors. What the hell does she really do?

He walked into this living room and pulled a Miles Davis from the record bin over his turntable, the soundtrack of a French New Wave film. Sanders loved that genre of film and thought his jazz performance was a perfect compliment.

He plopped down in his Eames lounger he had positioned near the sliding glass door. A small balcony overlooked a Visitor Parking area across the street from his building.

Sanders grimaced as he compared this view with

the one he had of downtown Dallas from the apartment he had leased the prior three years. He had only been in his townhome a few months and was seldom there during weekdays.

At 4:20 p.m., he decided to pour himself a glass of chardonnay and get some fresh air on his porch. Sanders walked to the edge of his balcony and looked right down the street in front of his townhouse.

A black Jaguar SUV was easing up the street toward Sanders. He surmised that the driver was trying to locate a particular address on his street.

The Jaguar inched past a parking space across the street and reversed, then maneuvered to parallel park in the space. A man in a dark suit, white shirt, and blue tie got out of the car.

Another corporate suit? What now?

Even though it was an overcast day, the man wore sunglasses and carried a black briefcase. As he walked toward Sanders' townhouse, his head rotated from side to side, while he surveyed his surroundings.

Sanders took a sip of wine and observed as the man made his way across the street. When he reached the other side, he paused to key a text message on his cell phone. After a few minutes, he slipped the phone back into his coat pocket and resumed walking in the direction of Sanders' townhouse.

Sanders watched the man step up to the porch of his next-door neighbor's unit. He leaned over the railing just as the man knocked on his neighbor's door. The man disappeared as his neighbor answered the door and let him inside.

I wonder if this guy is Claire's 4:30 p.m. appointment. What did she mean about power exchange?

Chapter 4

Wednesday at 1:00 p.m., Sanders drove the short distance to his gallery on Interurban Street. When he pulled into the parking lot in front, Taylor's car was parked in the space nearest the front door. Sanders parked next to her. As he walked toward the front door of his building, he waved at the security camera positioned on the eave of the roof near the door.

Taylor's voice came over the intercom. "Hi, Sanders."

Sanders laughed. "What are you doing spying on me from my office?"

Taylor left the intercom turned on, he suspected, so he could hear her laugh. He opened the door and walked into the gallery. All the gallery lights were lit. The artwork of several local artists adorned the walls.

Taylor rounded the corner into the main gallery. "We had some visitors today."

Sanders eyes lit up. "Excellent. Any prospective collectors?"

Taylor pointed to the other side of the gallery. "One woman really liked Genny's landscapes. She requested information on the artist, which is encouraging. Another woman came in and asked to see you."

Sanders wrinkled his forehead. "Really? Did she tell you her name?"

Taylor shook her head. "No, she didn't. I told her you usually come in around 2:00 p.m."

"What did she look like?"

"She was a tall thin brunette in her mid-thirties." Taylor paused and frowned, "She had a severe look about her and appeared to wear no or very little makeup."

"How was she dressed?"

"In a black suit, white shirt with black pumps, and matching black handbag."

"I can't imagine she'd be interested in anything colorful, then." Sanders sighed. "I have no idea who that might be. But it was great someone was curious about Genny's work."

Taylor nodded. "Yes, I think she'll be back."

"We've already had one sale this week," Sanders said. "If we can sell one of Genny's works, we'll set a new record."

Taylor laughed. "That would be nice. Then I guess you would have to give me a raise."

He smiled. "Believe it or not, that's exactly what I've been thinking about doing."

She narrowed her eyes, studying Sanders' face. "Are you serious?"

He gestured toward the office. "Let's go into the office and visit a few minutes."

Sanders followed Taylor to his office. She plopped

down in one of the client chairs. He walked around and sat in the other one instead of the chair behind his desk.

"Taylor, do you remember last week when I got that call from a former colleague offering me a temporary assignment?"

She nodded. "Yes. Are you going to take it?"

Sanders sighed. "At first, I was really hesitant about getting involved in some obscure corporate matter. After mulling it over awhile, I think I might do it. I'm not quite there yet. Also, I would really like to help Jackie, my former colleague. Have your job prospects changed since we last talked?"

Taylor rolled her eyes. "No. I haven't heard a peep from either UT or that gallery in Fort Worth."

He leaned forward in his chair. "Then would you consider working here full-time for a month or so while I do this job?"

She bounced in her chair. "Of course, you know I'll do it."

"Does an increase of ten dollars per hour," Sanders said, "and an expansion of hours to thirty a week sound reasonable?"

Taylor leaned over and gave him a hug. "Are you kidding? That's awesome! Can you afford to pay me that much?"

He snickered. "Only because I'll be getting paid a hefty amount if I take this temporary assignment."

She grinned. "Then you should definitely take the job."

Sanders glanced up at the monitor for the front door security camera on the wall behind Taylor. "It looks like we may have company."

The screen showed a woman sitting in her car parked in the place next to Sanders' Spider.

Sarah whipped her head around. "I think that's the woman who was in earlier asking to see you."

Sanders stood up. "Maybe we'll solve the identity of this mystery woman."

They both watched as the woman exited her car and walked over to the front door.

Taylor said, "Sanders, that's definitely her."

"Well then, let's go greet her in the gallery. Maybe she's here to see one of my paintings."

The front door buzzed as the woman entered the building. Sanders and Taylor rounded the corner into the main gallery. The woman was standing in the middle of the gallery, staring in their direction.

As they approached her, Sanders said, "Welcome to Interurban Contemporary. May we help you with something?"

The woman's stare was laser focused on Sanders. "Are you Charles Sanders Pierce?"

Sanders narrowed his eyes. He knew why Taylor described the woman as being severe.

He nodded. "Yes, I am Sanders Pierce."

She pulled out a badge from her coat pocket. "I'm Agent Angie Hale, FBI."

Sanders squinted to read the badge. "What can we do for you, Ms. Hale?"

Agent Hale slipped the badge back into her pocket. "May I talk in private with you, Mr. Sanders?"

"Sure, let's go into my office." He glanced over at Taylor. "Would you keep an eye on the gallery?"

Taylor nodded. "Of... of... course."

"Please follow me, Ms. Hale."

"Lead the way, Mr. Pierce."

Sanders led her to his office and closed the door behind them. He gestured with his right hand toward the nearest client chair. "Please have a seat."

He sat down in his desk chair. Having the desk separate the space between them gave him a slight sense of comfort. She slid into the client chair.

"Now, how can I be of any assistance to the FBI?"

Agent Hale pulled a black notebook out of her bag and flipped over a couple of pages. "I understand you've met with the General Counsel of Global Data Systems."

Sanders eyes widened. "Yes, I met with her this week."

She glanced down at her notebook. "To be precise, you met with her Tuesday afternoon."

He sighed. "That's correct. How did you know?"

"Mr. Pierce, the FBI has many ways of collecting information in an investigation."

Sanders stiffened in his chair. "Are you investigating me or Global Data Systems?"

"Relax, Mr. Pierce. You're not under investigation. Did the meeting with her concern the disclosure of personal health information?"

Sanders paused. "It involved a sensitive corporate matter."

She looked up from her notebook and said in a curt tone, "Was this 'sensitive corporate matter' related to the improper disclose of client health benefit information?"

His cheeks flushed. "Why don't you instead pose these questions to Jackie Rogers, the General Counsel?"

Agent Hale raised an eyebrow. "We're in the preliminary stage of the investigation. It's standard procedure to find out all the information available in advance before contacting the target. It's entirely possible that the investigation won't progress beyond the preliminary stage."

"Ms. Hale, I'm not comfortable disclosing what I discussed in confidence with Jackie Rogers."

She leaned forward, all but glaring at Sanders. "Not even to help the FBI determine if federal law was violated?"

Sanders sighed. "Not in this case."

Agent Hale slammed her notebook closed. "You do realize that I can have you served with a subpoena forcing you to talk to the FBI."

Sanders opened the top drawer to his desk and pulled out the offer from Global Data Systems.

"This envelope contains an offer to me from Global Data System to do short-term legal work on its behalf. My acceptance of this offer would prevent me from answering these questions, due to attorney client privilege."

She growled, "But you haven't signed it yet. Expect to be served with a subpoena."

Sanders took the offer out of the envelope, picked up a pen, signed, and dated the offer. "I have now, Ms. Hale."

Agent Hale shot to her feet. "I regret that you failed to cooperate."

Sander stood up. "I'll see you to the front door."

"I know the way out."

Agent Hale stormed out of his office with her heels reverberating on the concrete floor as she hurried toward the front door.

Sanders strolled out into the gallery and caught a glimpse of her as she exited the building.

He walked behind the bar on the left side of the gallery, opened the small refrigerator, and pulled out a bottle of chardonnay. As he was filling a wine glass, Taylor emerged from around the back corner. "Starting kind of early today, aren't you?"

Sanders chuckled. "I suppose I am."

Taylor plopped down on one the bar stools. "What did that FBI agent want?"

He took a swig of wine. "Care for a glass?"

She shook her head. "No, I'll wait a bit."

Sanders stared at his glass. "Agent Hale wanted to know what my meeting with Jackie Rogers at Global Data Systems was all about."

Taylor wrinkled her forehead. "What on earth for?"

"She said the FBI was conducting some preliminary investigation that may lead to a further in-depth investigation of Global Data Systems."

"Really. What are they investigating?"

He took another sip of wine. "My guess is the FBI is trying to determine whether Global Data Systems violated federal law."

Taylor's mouth dropped open. "Really! Why don't they just question someone at Global Data Systems?"

"Agent Hale said it's standard procedure for the FBI not to involve the potential target in the preliminary stage of an investigation."

"How did they even know you had a meeting there?"

Sanders smiled. "I have no clue whatsoever."

"Did you tell her anything about your meeting at Global Data Systems?"

He grimaced. "No, I told her I was not comfortable revealing the subject matter of my confidential conversation with Jackie."

Taylor's eyes widened. "I bet that went over well with Ms. Severe Look."

Sanders finished off his glass of wine. "Oh, she was not too happy with that response. She even threatened to subpoena me so I would be compelled to talk."

"How did you respond to that threat?"

He snickered. "I was a bit of a drama queen. I pulled the envelope out of my desk and told her that inside was an offer to perform legal work on behalf of

Global Data Systems. I informed her that if I signed it, my conversation with Jackie would be protected by attorney client privilege."

Taylor shifted her weight on the bar stool. "How did she take that?"

"She said I was still subject to be subpoenaed because I had yet to sign it. In a slight fit of rage, I pulled the offer out of the envelope and signed it right in front of her."

"You really showed her, didn't you?"

Sanders smiled. "Agent Hale expressed her regret that I wouldn't cooperate and then stormed out of my office. And do you know what's funny in hindsight?"

Taylor's eyes narrowed as she studied Sanders' face.

"I seriously doubt the attorney client privilege applies to conversations that occurred prior to when the client retained the attorney."

"I bet you're glad she didn't bring that possibility up."

He nodded. "I suppose she still could. I'll just have to wait and see if I'm subpoenaed."

Chapter 5

S anders arrived back his townhouse around 5:30 p.m. He noticed a package on his front porch as he pulled into his driveway.

After Sanders entered his house from the garage, he opened the front door and gazed down at the package with the Amazon logo on the outside. He could not remember ordering anything from Amazon in about a month.

Sanders brought the package inside and placed it on the credenza in a small room that he uses as an office on the first floor. He sliced through the packaging tape with some scissors and popped open the box.

What the hell is this?

Inside the inner packaging were three distinct types of black leather collars. He removed one of them so he could get a better look.

Are these dog collars? I didn't order this stuff.

Sanders put the collar back into the box and turned it over. He had not read the address label prior to opening it. The address on the label was that of his next-door neighbor.

Oh no, I opened Claire's package by mistake!

Sanders considered re-taping the box and leaving

it on Claire's porch but instead decided he would come clean and admit what happened. He took a couple of deep breaths before ringing her doorbell. After a couple of minutes, the bolt lock shifted and the doorknob turned.

Claire cracked the door open just enough to stick her head outside. She seemed puzzled when she recognized him. "Sanders?"

"Claire, I'm so sorry if I caught you at a bad time."

Claire opened the door a little wider. She was dressed the same way as when he first met her, outfitted in a black top, black yoga pants, and black runners. "What's up?"

Sanders gestured with his head toward the package. "When I got home this evening, I found this package on my porch. Unfortunately, I didn't read the label before opening it. I so apologize." He extended the package toward her.

She grabbed it and looked inside. "Oh, my collars have arrived."

Sanders wrinkled his forehead. "Do you have a dog?"

Claire looked up at him and through clenched teeth said, "No. I don't."

His eyes widened. "Okay. Anyway, I'm sorry I opened your package by mistake. I'll be more careful next time."

"I would appreciate that."

Sanders took a step backwards. "Have a good evening."

She forced a smile and nodded before closing the door.

Sanders felt terrible for having opened his neighbor's package. He pondered what else he could do to make amends.

I don't want my next-door neighbor to hate me!

Chapter 6

Sanders was due at Global Data Systems Monday at 9:00 a.m. Before he left for the short commute north, he put a bottle of 2018 Quintessa Cabernet Sauvignon in a small gift bag and leaned it near his next-door neighbor's front door. Within the bag was a brief note apologizing for opening her package the day before. He had just purchased the bottle of wine at retail pricing for around two hundred dollars. If Claire knew anything about wine, she would realize it was a considerate gift.

Sanders hopped in his Spider and was on the North Dallas Tollway in a matter of minutes. He pulled up to the Security Gate and flashed the badge that Jackie Rogers had overnighted to him. The guard waved him through.

He found a parking place right away and made his way up to the building on day one of his new temporary assignment. Jackie had told him to come straight to where her office was located and her secretary, Beverly, would get him situated in his new office. He arrived on the tenth floor at 8:55 a.m. on the dot.

Beverly met him as he exited the elevator. "Good morning, Mr. Pierce."

"Good morning, Beverly."

Beverly pressed the elevator button. "We're going back down to the first floor. Your office will be in Sector G."

When they stepped off the elevator on the first floor, Sanders was struck by the noticeable difference in ambiance from the tenth floor. The walls were painted gray, which matched the thin industrial-grade carpet. Dark blue cubicles lined the exterior walls.

The route to Sector G was circuitous

Sanders said, "This is quite a maze."

Beverly nodded. "Yes, especially since everything looks alike."

Ten minutes later they arrived at a closed door marked G-35. Beverly slipped a key into the door-knob, unlocked the door, and switched on the lights. "This is your office. I'm afraid it's a little small."

Sanders guessed it to be about ten feet by twelve feet. It was furnished with a gray laminated desk and matching credenza. Behind the desk was a dark blue desk chair and in front, two dark blue client chairs. No artwork adorned the walls. A personal computer and telephone sat on top of the desk. Stacks of files were piled on top of the credenza.

"This is a bit cozy. But it's fine for my purposes."

She pointed at the files on the credenza. "Those files contain the materials that you and Ms. Rogers discussed."

"That should keep me busy for a while."

Beverly picked up the phone receiver and listened for a dial tone. "Your phone number is 972-605-3381." She gestured toward the laptop computer. "Your login identification is 'szym92'. When you log on the first time, you will be prompted to set up a password."

Sanders sat down behind the desk. "That sounds simple enough."

"Your email address is S.Pierce@GDS.com," Beverly said. "Your initial password for email is 'investigation'. Please change it after you logon one time."

Sanders rubbed his chin. "Will do."

She took a step backwards. "I think that's all. Do you have any questions?"

He shook his head. "No, I'm going to get acquainted with my computer and then focus on the files."

"If you need anything, feel free to give me a call. My direct number is 605-3555."

"Thank you, Beverly."

Sanders signed into his email as instructed and reset his password to 'Shelly123'. He had dated a girl named Shelly throughout high school. She was a year older than Sanders and broke up with him when she went off to college. Over the years Sanders had often used the names of past girlfriends in various passwords.

When he accessed his email, his eyebrows shot up. He already had an email from someone identified only as System Administrator, welcoming him to his account and reminding him to change his initial password. Sanders spent the better part of the day focusing the account involved in the leaked health information. He familiarized himself with the organization chart and the various responsibilities allocated from top to the lowest ranking employee.

Next, Sanders studied a detailed workflow laying out the various steps of how a health claim gets processed by Global Data Systems.

At 5:00 p.m., someone knocked on his office door. He hurried over to the door and swung it open.

Jackie Rogers was standing outside. She smiled. "How's it going?"

"Hi, Jackie, please come in." He gestured toward the closest client chair. "Have a seat in one of my plastic chairs."

She groaned. "Sorry, Sanders, but the furniture and office size are a bit different from private practice."

Sanders grinned. "Just kidding. Everything's fine."

Jackie plopped down in one of client chairs. "Beverly said she got you oriented with your computer, email, and phone.

"Yep, all good."

"Have you had a chance to review all the materials we assembled for you?"

Sanders pointed at a lone file at the edge of his desk. "I just have that last one to go through and then I'll be ready for phase two."

She leaned forward. "What's your plan for phase two?"

"I'm going to schedule interviews. Assuming I get cooperation from everyone, I would like to begin at the bottom of the claims processing flow chart and work my way up."

Jackie shifted in her seat. "Did you see the email I copied you on that I sent to the manager of the affected account?"

He shook his head. "No, I haven't been on email since early this morning."

"For starters, I directed him to appoint a gate-keeper as your contact for the account. If you want to talk to some employee in the account, you simply reach out to the gatekeeper, who will make it happen."

"Great. That should make the whole process work better."

She nodded. "Yes, I thought that was the best way to handle it."

"What about the incentive we discussed in our initial meeting?"

Jackie sighed. "You mean offering a financial incentive to come forward with information?"

He tapped the desk with his forefinger. "Yes, I think it might help."

"Let's see how it goes without doing that at first. We can always revisit it a little bit later."

"Okay, that's fine."

"Anything else you need from me at this time?"

He leaned back in his chair. "No, I think I'm good

for the moment."

She stood up. "I'll let you get back to it."

"Have a good evening, Jackie."

"You, too." Jackie closed the door behind her.

Sanders went through the final file page by page. He glanced at his watch. It was 5:45 p.m. He had not worked a full day since he left private practice. Before calling it a day, he accessed his email.

Two messages appeared in his inbox. The first one was the carbon copy from Jackie of the email she sent to management. He read it and set up a GDS file on his computer and moved the email to the file.

The second email was from a EmmaPeel22gmail. com. He chuckled.

Emma Peel of the Avengers fame? I loved Mrs. Peel when I was a kid! That's obviously a fake name.

The email had no subject. Sanders accessed it. It read:

Caution! Things are not always as they seem!

He was the sole recipient of the email No one was carbon-copied on it. Sanders scratched his head.

Is this for real or some kind prank?

Chapter 7

Sanders pulled his car into the garage and went around front to check to see if he had any mail. Resting on top of a stack of bills and advertisements was a sealed blank envelope. He fished it out and ripped it open. Inside was a note from his next-door neighbor.

> Sanders, Thank you for the exquisite bottle of wine. I happen to know a 2018 Quintessa Cabernet Sauvignon set you back a few dollars. It really was not necessary, but I appreciate the gesture. Care to share a glass with me later this evening?
> Shall we say 7:30 p.m.? - C.

Sanders smiled. *Well, at least my neighbor doesn't hate me.*

He went inside his townhouse, changed into blue jeans and a sport shirt, and fixed himself a dinner of pasta with bolognaise sauce. If he was going to join Claire for a glass of wine, he might as well enjoy a glass of cabernet with dinner.

At the stroke of 7:30 p.m., Sanders exited his townhouse and took the few steps south to his neighbor's front door. He rang the doorbell. A few minutes passed before Claire answered the door. She was wearing her usual black shirt, yoga pants, and matching runners.

"Right on time. I just opened the Quintessa to let it breathe."

"Excellent."

Claire swung the door wide open. "Please come in."

He walked inside the entry hall. The layout of the townhouse was a mirror version of his place. She locked the door behind them and led him upstairs to the second floor where the living room, dining room, and kitchen were located. The second story had a different kind of wood laminate than his floor.

"How long have you lived here, Claire?"

She wrinkled her nose. "Just over four years."

"The place looks great. Did you have to do any remodeling?"

Claire nodded. "Extensively, especially upstairs." She took a step towards the small kitchen. "Let me get us some wine glasses."

He watched as she pulled two wine glasses from the wooden cabinet next to the range top. The granite on the kitchen counters was an unusual, marbled earth tone color.

"Beautiful counter tops. I don't think I've ever seen this kind of granite before."

She grimaced. "It's quite unusual and, unfortunately, quite expensive."

Resting on top of the bar that separated the kitchen from the dining room, he spotted the three collars from the package that he had opened yesterday.

Claire poured two glasses of wine and handed one to him. "Salute."

"Cheers." Sanders waited for her to take the first sip.

She sniffed the glass before taking a healthy swig. He followed suit and said, "What do you think?"

Her eyes widened. "It's quite lovely."

He smiled. "This is only the second time I've tasted a Quintessa. The first time was in California a couple of years ago. I just fell in love with it, despite the hefty price."

Claire nodded. "I can understand why."

Sanders gestured toward the collars. "I'm still embarrassed that I opened your package by mistake."

"No worries, Sanders. This wine more than makes up for it."

He smiled. "If I'm not prying, can you tell me what the collars are for?"

Her eyes narrowed. "I use them in my therapy."

Sanders raised an eyebrow. "Really? Can you elaborate?"

She set her glass on the counter and picked up a thick leather collar. "Turn around."

He did as Claire instructed. She slipped the collar snuggly around Sanders" neck and gave a tug on the metal loop that is designed to attach to a leash. As his neck muscles tightened, he twisted around to face

Claire, almost spilling his wine.

Claire cackled. "Surprised?"

A chill shot down his spine. "Quite surprised. But how can this be part of your therapy?"

"Remember I told you part of my therapy involves power exchange."

Sanders let out an audible gulp. "Yes. This is part of psychotherapy?"

She nodded. "Of course. Don't you feel a little vulnerable wearing that collar?"

He reached up and touch the collar with his free hand. "I suppose I do."

Claire grabbed the metal ring on the collar. "Can you imagine how you would feel if I attached a leash to your collar?"

"You do that in therapy?"

Claire growled. "If the situation calls for it."

Sanders set his wine glass down and fiddled with the buckle of the collar.

"Relax, Sanders. Turn around and I'll unbuckle it."

He turned around and exhaled when she removed the collar.

She whispered in his ear. "Much better, right."

Sanders whirled back around. "Yes. I wasn't expecting that."

Claire chuckled. "It's interesting how you can turn the tables on someone in a matter of seconds."

He wrinkled his forehead. "What do you do after you slip a collar and leash on someone?" He pointed to two leather chairs facing one another across the room. "Do you just sit down over there and talk?"

She shook her head. "No, all kinds of scenarios can be played out. But I don't do therapy in my living room." Her eyes glanced upward. "I do that in my spare room upstairs."

Sanders knew which room she was referencing, since his unit was identical.

"I see. What else do—"

"That's enough talk about my therapy for the evening."

He nodded. "Of course. I'm just fascinated by it all."

She smiled. "Well, maybe I'll give you a tour of my playroom sometime."

He gasped. "Playroom?"

She walked over and picked up the bottle of wine. "That's just what I call it. Care for a refill?"

Sanders twisted his mouth into a half-smile. "If I say 'yes', will I have to wear that collar?"

Claire snickered. "No, I've had my fun." She poured them both a glass of wine. "So, what do you do for a living, Sanders?"

He paused to consider how to answer. "Well, I practiced law for most of my adult life but have since transitioned to being a visual artist."

"Really? That's quite a transition." She handed him his glass of wine.

He took the glass. "Thank you. It's a long story but I soured on practicing law."

She gestured toward the two leather chairs with her left hand. "Care to have a seat?"

Sanders slid into one of the chairs and Claire into the other. "So, do you paint as a hobby, or do you consider it a profession?"

He sighed. "The latter but sometimes it feels more like a hobby. However, I do have a nice studio and gallery."

Her eyebrows shot up. "Really? That sounds quite professional to me. Where's your gallery located?"

"Ever heard of Interurban Drive just east of Central Expressway?"

Claire shook her head. "No, I'm not familiar with it."

"The street is lined with used car dealerships and repair shops." He smirked at her. "I thought it would be a perfect spot for an art gallery. Wouldn't you agree?"

She snickered. "Well, sometimes it's good to be a pioneer. I'll have to come by and check it out."

Sanders took a sip of wine. "That would be great. Unfortunately, I'm on a sabbatical of sorts now. I just agreed to take a temporary legal position with a large corporation."

"That doesn't sound as much fun as art."

"My former colleague is now general counsel there. She asked if I could help on a matter in which I have a bit of expertise. So, I agreed to do it."

She finished off her glass of wine. "I'm sure she's very appreciative."

Sanders checked his watch. "It's late, and I should let you enjoy the rest of your evening. Thank you so much for inviting me over to share this phenomenal cabernet."

Claire kidded. "Bring me another bottle of Quintessa and you have yourself a date."

He laughed. "That's a deal."

As Sanders made the quick trek next door to his townhouse, he could not get over Claire's description of where she gives therapy as a playroom.

What kind of therapy does she provide?

Chapter 8

The next morning, Sanders parked his Spider and entered Global Data Systems. It took him almost ten minutes to weave his way through the maze of cubicles and hallways before he arrived at G-35. He unlocked the door to his office and plopped down in his chair. He switched on his P.C. and entered his username, szym92, and his password, Shelly123.

The only email was from Jackie Rogers sent thirty minutes earlier.

> Just F.Y.I., I have just been alerted that we now have a second account where private health information has been improperly leaked. We received a letter from the alleged victim's attorney. As soon as Corporate Security investigates, I will brief you this afternoon on what we have learned. Jackie

Sanders pulled out the file on the Beta Account. *Might as well start at the beginning.*

He studied the flowchart for claims processing. *I need to understand what happens once a claim is received by the account. Probably a long shot but there must be a breach in the system somewhere along the line.*

Sanders called the individual who was his designated gatekeeper for the account. He said he wanted to interview Jon Moran, who oversaw the mail room and scanning of incoming documents. Sanders surmised that the scanning of the claims and supporting information was the first possible opportunity for the whole process to be breached.

Within twenty minutes, someone knocked at his office door. Sanders opened the door. A Black man in his late twenties, dressed in the corporate appropriate white shirt, charcoal gray suit, and matching tie, said, "Mr. Pierce?"

"Yes, I'm Sanders. Please come in and have a seat."

Once they both were settled, Sanders said, "Please tell me your name and position in the Beta Account."

The man took a deep breath before answering. Sanders speculated he was trying to calm his nerves.

"I'm Jon Moran, Supervisor of Receipt, Scanning and Encryption Operations."

Sanders knew the answer but wanted to set the line of questioning. "Tell me as precisely as possible how the whole workflow process works that you supervise."

Jon leaned forward in his chair. "Each morning, we examine all received mail to make sure Beta is the appropriate destination within Global Data Systems. Once that determination is made, all materials are sent to be scanned."

Sanders gestured with his pen. "Do you sort the information before scanning. For example, you might receive a claim filed by the health plan participant, and in other cases, it may be information from a health care provider."

Jon shook his head. "No, we scan it all without sorting."

Sanders jotted down some notes. "So, I would assume there's no need for anyone at this stage of process to actually read any of the materials received."

"That's correct, other than making sure that Beta is the appropriate destination."

Sanders leaned back in his chair. "What happens next?"

"Once the scanning process is completed, all records are encrypted. Global Data Systems developed the software that reads the scanned records and encrypts them."

"How many operators are involved in this process?"

Jon held up three fingers. "Three, to be exact."

Sanders glanced down at his legal pad. "Could one of these three people read the scanned records if they so desired?"

Jon shook his head. "Possible, but highly unlikely. In most organizations the size of Beta, four people are typically necessary to perform this function. As you might suspect, Global Data Systems likes to maximize resources. In other words, none of these three operators would have the luxury of time to read anything."

Sanders narrowed his eyes. "Let's take a step back. What happens to the original documentation after it is scanned?"

Jon sighed. "After encryption, the original documentation is placed in large envelopes that are sealed and then filed away in storage by Corporate Security. A Corporate Security person is always present to monitor this process, along with three strategically positioned security cameras. And before you ask, no one reads the original documentation before it's stored."

"Who has access to the stored files?"

Jon pointed up with his right index finger. "The head of Corporate Security."

"Okay, once the records are encrypted and stored in the server, do you have any more responsibility for them?"

"Nada."

Sanders jotted on his legal pad and then looked up. "Jon, you obviously know what I'm here to investigate, correct?"

He nodded. "Of course, everyone does."

"Where do you think the breach took place?"

Jon shrugged. "I don't have a clue."

Sanders sighed. "Okay, thanks for your time."

Jon stood up and headed toward the door. "Would you like me to close the door behind me?"

"Yes, thanks."

Sanders checked his watch. It was 11:30 a.m. He decided to log onto his email.

The first email was from Jackie, setting up a brief meeting with him this afternoon. She requested to meet in Sanders' office. He responded, confirming the meeting.

The second email was from Stevie Greene. Stevie requested a meeting with Sanders to discuss a confidential matter. Sanders picked up the organizational chart and searched for her name. Although, this was not where he wanted to go next in his investigation, he agreed to schedule a meeting with her at 1:00 p.m.

Sanders returned from lunch at 12:45 p.m. Promptly at 1:00 p.m., a faint knock came on his office door. Sanders sprung to his feet and opened the door. A petite, young brunette dressed in a black pantsuit and pink shirt was standing there straight ahead.

Sanders said, "You must be Stevie Greene."

She nodded. "Yes sir."

Sanders gestured with his right hand. "Please come in and have a seat."

He closed the door behind him and ambled around to his chair behind the desk. "I'm Sanders Pierce. As I think you know, I've been retained on temporary assignment by Global Data Systems to investigate some leaks of client health information."

Stevie nodded. "Yes sir, I know."

Sanders picked up the organizational chart. "It appears you're in Batching of Records and Files."

Instead of making eye contact, she stared at the organization chart in his hand. "Yes sir, I'm a key operator."

He picked up his pen. "What exactly is a key operator?"

Stevie fidgeted in her chair. "I key in validated claims into the client's claims adjudication system."

"I see. You indicated in your email that you had a confidential matter you wanted to discuss with me."

Her eyes darted around the office, scanning the area as if checking for a security camera. "Yes, sir. I don't think we are keying in all validated claims."

Sanders eyes narrowed. "What do you mean?"

"I'm not going to get in trouble for talking to you, am I?"

He leaned back in his chair. "I've been assured by your General Counsel that no one will face any kind of repercussions for talking to me. You can report any problems you have straight to Legal Affairs."

She swallowed. "Tom Saunders is a key operator also. I share a cubicle with him. Every so often, I can see out of my peripheral vision that he seems to drop a record, claim, or whatever into the left bottom drawer of his desk instead of keying it in and placing it in the outgoing file."

"He *seems* to drop these items into his drawer. Are you less than certain he drops these items in his drawer?"

Stevie shook her head. "No, I'm not absolutely certain."

Sanders shifted in his chair. "Have you said anything to him about it?"

"No, I'm afraid to say anything."

He wrinkled his forehead. "Why would you be afraid to ask him?"

She sniffled. "I know our manager would believe him over me, regardless of whether he was found to have done something wrong."

"Why would management believe him if he did something wrong?"

"Jack and my manager are both veterans. Tom suffers a disability from a wound he received in Afghanistan. Because of his disability, he's a little slow. He often makes mistakes when he keys in items, but our manager covers for him constantly."

Sanders rubbed his bald head. "What's the name of your manager?"

Stevie sighed. "Fred Stiers."

"Okay, is there anything else?"

She shook her head. "No. What are you going to do next?"

Sanders leaned back in his chair. "I'm going to schedule an interview with Fred Stiers."

Her eyes widened, as she gasped. "You're not going to tell him what I said, are you?"

"Don't worry. I'll be discreet."

Stevie stood up and walked toward the door.

"Please close the door behind you," he called to her.

Sanders logged into his account and found an

email from Beverly. She said Jackie wanted to meet with him at 2:30 p.m. in his office. He glanced at the right-hand lower corner of his computer screen for the time. It was 2:10 p.m.

Sanders wanted to schedule an appointment with Fred Stiers, but he was uncertain how long the meeting with Jackie would take. So, he emailed the gatekeeper and asked for an interview to be scheduled with Fred Stiers for 9:00 a.m. the following morning. Next, he logged into the Global Data Systems database listing the employees and searched for the name of the head of Corporate Security. If Jackie approved, he wanted to schedule an interview with him.

At 2:15 p.m., another knock came on his office door. Jackie entered his office before he could respond and closed the door behind her. She walked over and plopped down in the nearest client chair.

Sanders said, "You look like you've had a bad day."

Jackie sighed. "And it's not over yet. How's your investigation going?"

He leaned back in his chair. "I'm trying to not go down rabbit holes. However, I may have to do just that to make sure I don't miss something. Also, you said there's another leak of health information."

She frowned. "Yes, this time with the Gamma Account. Global Data Systems has only three accounts that handle health benefit claims administration, and there has now been at a breach in the Beta Account *and* the Gamma Account. So far, we're not aware of anything from the Delta Account. I say at least one breach in each of those accounts, because there may be others that have not been brought to our attention."

"Do you know the nature of the medical information that was leaked this time?"

Jackie shook her head. "Not yet. The letter we received from an attorney representing a plan participant just identified it as sensitive confidential medical information. We know the name of the participant and which health plan he was enrolled in. Corporate Security is looking into it now."

Sanders leaned forward. "Would it be possible for me to interview the head of Corporate Security?"

She wrinkled her forehead. "I suppose so, since he reports directly to me. But why him?"

"I just want to tie up a loose end."

"His name's Allen Collins. I'll give him a call in the morning."

Sanders scratched his head. "Also, could I see a copy of the attorney's letter?"

She glanced down at her watch. "Of course. I'll have Beverly send one to you. I've a meeting in five minutes, so I need to hurry."

"Thank you."

Jackie stood up. "We'll keep you updated on the Gamma matter as we receive more information. I'm sure you've plenty to do on the other account."

He smiled. "Yes, I haven't scratched the surface yet."

Sanders thought about telling Jackie about the mysterious Emma Peel email but opted to remain silent on the subject until he could research further. He watched as she closed the office door behind her.

* * *

As Sanders eased the Spider into his driveway, he noticed a piece of paper taped to his front door. He parked his car in the garage and went inside his townhouse. He crossed over to his front door, opened it, and removed the paper. It was a note from Claire. It read:

> Hey neighbor, if you get home by 6:00 p.m., why don't you join me at the bar at Cappuccino's for a glass or two of wine. I might even have dinner.
> -Claire

Sanders had dined alone at Cappuccino's Italian Bistro several times. It was a five-minute walk from his front door to the restaurant. He glanced at his watch. It was 5:50 p.m.

I think I'll take Claire up on her offer!

Sanders rushed upstairs and dropped off his briefcase and hurried back downstairs. He arrived at Cappuccino's a few minutes later.

Upon entering the restaurant, he spotted Claire sitting at the bar. She was dressed in her customary black top, but instead of yoga pants, she wore blue jeans. Her black hair was pulled back into a ponytail.

Claire appeared to be visiting with the bartender, who hovered near her from behind the bar. When Sanders approached the bar, the bartender straightened up.

Claire swiveled her head to the right and smiled at Sanders. "Ah, neighbor, I didn't know if you would be able to make it."

He dragged out the chair next to where she was sitting and plopped down on it.

"Yes, I saw your note when I pulled up to my place. Thanks for inviting me to join you."

"Of course."

The bartender said to Sanders, "May I bring you something to drink?"

Claire gestured toward her wine glass. "It's no Quintessa Cabernet, but the house chianti is rather good."

Sanders said, "I'll have a glass of what she's having."

They both watched as the bartender pulled a bottle of chianti from under the bar and poured a glass. He set the glass on a napkin in front of Sanders and said, "Claire, would you care for me to top yours off?"

She nodded. "Sure, why not?"

Sanders sniffed and then took a sip of wine. "You must be a regular here."

"I come here about twice a month. How about

you? Have you been here before?"

He nodded. "Several times, especially when I first moved in."

She took a sip of wine. "How do you like living in our quaint little community?"

"I think I'm going to enjoy living here." Sanders said with a chuckle. "I can say one thing for certain, I have a very interesting next-door neighborhood."

Claire's eyes widened. "Why do you find me so interesting?"

He flipped the end of his cocktail napkin. "I don't know. I just find you a bit mysterious."

She sighed. "Okay, if you say so. By the way, don't you think you're a little bit mysterious also. You're an attorney who turned artist who is now on a secret assignment with a large corporation."

He grinned. "Okay, let's agree that we're both a bit mysterious then."

* * *

Sanders and Claire decided also to have dinner at Cappuccino's. After dinner they strolled back to their townhouses. When they rounded the corner, a man dressed in a dark suit, white shirt, and gray tie leaned against a streetlight right across from Sanders' townhouse. Illuminated by the streetlight, he stood motionless, staring down Grove Park Lane, holding a large envelope in his left hand.

Sanders glanced over at Claire. "See that guy

down the street?"

"Yelp. He looks out of place. God, I hope he's not one of my clients."

"Did you have an appointment scheduled for tonight?"

She shook her head. "No. But I've had clients show up unannounced before."

As they drew closer, the man stepped out from underneath the light and crossed the street. He was now in front of their two townhouses.

When Sanders and Claire were a few feet from him, the man said, "Good evening."

Sanders said, "Good evening."

The man said, "Are you Charles Sanders Pierce?"

Sanders froze. "May I ask who you are?"

The man walked up to Sanders and handed him the envelope. "Mr. Sanders, I'm a process server and you've just been served with a subpoena."

The man turned around and strode down Grove Park Lane in the opposite direction.

Claire's mouth dropped open.

Sanders said, "I was kind of halfway expecting this to happen."

He walked up on his porch so he could see better under his porch light, and Claire followed. Sanders slid his thumb under the flap of the envelope and ripped it open. One by one, he removed the contents, which consisted of three pages.

Sanders groaned louder. "It's a subpoena from the FBI."

She touched his shoulder. "Why is the FBI subpoenaing you?"

He glanced down at the subpoena. "It has to do with the corporate assignment I'm on."

Claire raised an eyebrow. "Really? What do they want you to do?"

"I have to be deposed at the FBI's Dallas headquarters on Thursday at 10:00 a.m. Crap, that's this week!"

She gestured with her head. "Care to come in for a glass of wine?"

Sanders sighed. "Thank you, Claire. That would be nice."

Claire unlocked the door to her townhouse and Sanders followed her upstairs to the second floor living room area.

He said, "Do you mind if I take a few minutes to read this subpoena."

She shook here her. "Not at all. I'll pour us a glass of wine."

Sanders slid into one of the loungers and switched on the table light. Claire returned from the kitchen and set a glass of wine down next to him.

"Thank you, Claire."

She sat in the other recliner next to Sanders. After a couple of minutes, Sanders folded the subpoena and placed it back in the envelope.

Claire took a sip of wine. "May I ask what kind of information the FBI is seeking from you?"

Sanders grimaced. "I'm afraid the subpoena

forbids me from discussing it with anyone. I suspect the FBI wants to keep its involvement secret for the time being."

She clinked his glass of wine setting on the table with her glass. "Try a taste of your wine."

He picked up his glass, sniffed it, and took a swallow of wine. "A nice cab. What is it?"

"It's a 2019 Camus. One of my favorites."

Sanders smiled. "You have excellent taste for a mysterious woman."

Claire snickered. "I'm mysterious? Hell, you're the one who gets served a subpoena which forbids you to even discuss it with anyone. I would call that mysterious."

He laughed. "You make an excellent point. I'm curious. Have you had an opportunity to use one of your new collars in a therapy session yet?"

She set her wine glass down on the table. "As a matter of fact, I incorporated the thick leather one, the same one you modeled for me, in a session this afternoon."

His eyebrows shot up. "Really! You've got to give me some specifics sometime of exactly what you do in these sessions."

Claire finished off her glass of wine. "Perhaps sometime. But not tonight."

Sanders glanced down at her empty glass and then drained his own. He shifted in his chair and prepared to stand up. "Thanks so much for everything this evening. I really enjoyed it."

She smiled. "I enjoyed it as well."

Sanders stood up. "Well, I better get out of your hair and let you get on with the rest of your evening."

She joined him in standing. "What are your plans for the rest of the evening?"

He gave her a wry smile. "I'll probably spend the remainder of the evening reading and re-reading the subpoena."

Sanders made the short trek over to his front door.

Claire's right. I'm involved in some pretty mysterious stuff!

Chapter 9

Wednesday morning at 8:15 a.m., Sanders logged into his Global Data Systems email account. He had only one new email confirming his appointment in forty-five minutes with Fred Stiers, the Manager of Batching of Records and Files. Sanders often wondered how people ended up in their respective careers. Did Fred Stiers dream of being the Manager of Batching of Records and Files as a child?

Someone gave three rapid knocks to Sanders' office door at 8:55 a.m.

Sanders said, "Please come in."

A lean, squared-jawed man with a crew cut, dressed in a charcoal gray suit, white shirt, and navy-blue tie, opened the door and shut it behind him. "I assumed you wanted the door closed."

Sanders gestured with his right hand toward his client chairs. "Please have a seat."

Sanders waited for the man to get settled in a client chair. "You must be Fred Stiers."

"Yes, I'm Stiers."

Sanders picked up his pen and twirled it with his right hand. It was a habit he picked up from his days as a trial attorney. "I'm Sanders Pierce. I'm here—"

"I know who you are, Mr. Pierce, and why you're here."

"Okay, I guess we can dispense with the introductions then. I see from the flow chart that you're the Beta Account's Manager of Batching and Records."

Fred stared down at the legal pad in front of Sanders. "That's correct."

"Can you tell me about your job?"

Fred shifted in his chair. "I oversee all the operators to make sure all the decrypted information received in the system from Decryption gets securely keyed on the client's claims adjudication system."

Sanders jotted on his legal pad. "So, the health information is received from one system and then it is keyed into the various clients' health benefit plans, correct?"

Fred nodded. "That's correct."

"Please tell me how many operators are under your management."

"Eight."

Sanders leaned back in his chair. "Do all these operators work side by side?"

Fred wrinkled his forehead. "Do you mean do they sit physically next to one another?"

"Yes."

Fred sighed. "Two operators share a cubicle, making four separate enclosed cubicles."

Sanders set his pen down. "If I understand correctly, then the operators cannot observe what happens in the other cubicles?"

"That's true. Even the ones who share a cubicle would have a tough time seeing what the other one does."

Sanders eyes narrowed. "Wouldn't it be possible to look over and observe what the other operator is doing?"

Fred shook his head. "That's not humanly possible. To avoid distractions, there is a partition between the two operators and each sit with his or her back against that partition. There is no way an operator could see what the other one is doing."

"What if one stood up to, say, go to the restroom. Couldn't he see at least peek at what the other one is doing? For example, couldn't one operator see if the other operator was slipping sheets of data in his desk drawer instead of entering it into the system?"

"Of course. In fact, I have two operators who are instructed to do that very thing."

Sanders raised an eyebrow. "Why?"

Fred leaned forward. "Mr. Pierce, I have two veterans in my group. Both have disabilities. They are fine men but a little slow. They are allowed to pace themselves. Each works overtime to catch up."

"How are you sure then that all the information actually gets entered in the system?" Sanders jotted more on his legal pad.

Fred sneered. "Because there are safeguards in place. All the data that leaves the decryption process must match exactly as that entered into the system by the operators. It's part of my job to make sure there are no discrepancies."

Sanders straightened up in his chair. "And who makes sure that you've done your job correctly?"

"My manager. Who do you think?" Fred snapped. "Everything's automated and verified by software designed for this specific purpose. There's no room for error."

"I see." Sanders sighed. "Is there an image of how the operator's cubicles are structured?"

"It's on Global Data Systems' internal website."

"Great. That is all I need for now, Fred. Thank you for your time."

Fred shot to his feet and left without responding. He slammed the office door behind him.

Sanders accessed the Global Data Systems internal website and located an image of the cubicles layout in Batching of Records and Files. It was exactly as Fred described.

Stevie Greene's account of the whole matter is inconsistent with reality. I unwittingly just got lured down my first rabbit hole!

Chapter 10

O n Thursday morning at 9:45 a.m., Sanders drove his Spider to the Dallas FBI headquarters located on Justice Way in northwest Dallas. Sanders thought it was curious that the address had no numbers. He assumed the headquarters occupied all of Justice Way, dispensing with the need to have numbers in the address.

He edged up to the main gate and a uniformed security guard asked to see his identification. Sanders fished his wallet out of his coat pocket and handed his license to the guard. The guard disappeared with the license into a small structure near the gate. After a few minutes he emerged and handed the license back to Sanders and opened the gate so that Sanders could drive onto the property.

He eased the Spider into a large parking lot and followed the signs to Visitor Parking. The headquarters was a five-story building which appeared to have been built in the 1990s. He never knew it existed until he received the subpoena and conducted an internet search to see where the deposition was to take place.

Sanders strolled up to the front entrance and went through the revolving front glass door. As soon as he entered, he was required to go through a metal detector like those used in airports. When he cleared security, a guard jerked his head toward the center of the foyer. "She'll get you checked in."

Sanders checked in with the receptionist, who handed him a Visitor Badge. He clipped it on the top left pocket of his sport coat and located a chair in the small reception area facing the elevators. Two uniformed Richardson police officers were seated to his left and a single man dressed in a tan suit, blue shirt, and red tie was to his right.

Ten minutes later, the elevator chimed and opened. A woman dressed in a blue suit and white shirt exited the elevator and approached the officers. She said, "Gentlemen, please follow me."

Sanders watched as the doors of the elevator closed behind the two officers and the woman. He glanced at his watch. It was 10:20 a.m.

God, I hope this deposition doesn't last too long!

Ten minutes later the elevator chimed, and Agent Angie Hale exited and made a beeline to where Sanders was sitting. Sanders sprang to his feet and waited for her to draw near.

She wore a fierce expression, which softened a bit as she made eye contact with Sanders. "Thank you for coming, Mr. Pierce."

Sanders considered a sarcastic response but thought the better of it. "You're welcome, Agent Hale."

She motioned with her left hand toward the elevator. "Please, after you. We'll be going to the fourth floor."

With the agent following, Sanders walked in the direction of the elevator and they passed through its open doors. When the elevator arrived at the fourth floor, she said, "We'll be in Conference Room 444.

Please follow me."

Sanders was surprised under the circumstances she was even this cordial, given that she was a bit brusque. The door to Conference Room 444 was open when they arrived. Two men were seated behind a long maple table facing the door. Both were dressed in charcoal gray suits, white shirts, and dark ties. They looked the textbook version of FBI agents.

The man on the left was tall, thin, pale skin with thick white hair, and appeared to be in his fifties. The man on the right was much younger, Black with chiseled features and short hair.

Agent Hale gestured first toward the man on the left. "This is Agent Morton, and this is Agent Lee."

Both men nodded as they were introduced. Agent Hale walked around the right side of the table and sat next to Agent Lee. Sanders sat opposite the three of them. As soon as they were seated, Agent Hale pressed an intercom button on the device sitting in the middle of the table. "Please send in the court reporter."

A young twenty-something woman entered the room, carrying her digital recording machine.

Her gray pantsuit is predictable, but the yellow blouse is a nice change.

She sat down at the end of the table on Sanders' right and appeared meticulous as she set up her machine. When she was finished, she looked over at the agents. "Shall I swear in the witness?"

Agent Lee said, "Please."

She turned and faced Sanders. "Please raise your right hand."

Sanders complied with the request.

"Do you solemnly swear or affirm that the testimony you are about to give is the truth and nothing but the truth?"

Sanders said, "Yes."

Each agent had a legal pad on the table in front of them. Agent Lee said, "Mr. Sanders, I'm an attorney and will be handling the questions today. To begin, could you please state your full name, for the record."

"Charles Sanders Pierce."

"What city and county do you reside?"

Sanders leaned forward. "Richardson, Dallas County."

Agent Lee's eyes were laser-focused on Sanders. "What do you do for a living?"

Sanders hesitated to search for the best way to respond. "I spent most of my adult life practicing law, but now I'm pretty much retired from law and have transitioned to being a visual artist."

"So, you no longer practice law?"

Sanders sighed. "That's not entirely true. I've been retained for a temporary assignment with Global Data Systems."

Agent Lee stiffened in his chair. "So, you've been retained as legal counsel by Global Data Systems?"

Sanders nodded. "Yes, I was hired to do an internal investigation on the corporation's behalf."

"I presume that Global Data Systems is a Fortune 100 corporation. Why would it find the need to hire a retired attorney?"

"I used to practice law with Jackie Rogers, who is now Global Data Systems' General Counsel. She was aware of my expertise as a health benefits attorney."

Agent Lee squinted at Sanders. "That still doesn't

answer my question. There must be thousands of attorneys with that type of expertise with major firms throughout the United States. Why would she contact you?"

Sanders took a deep breath. "As I've indicated, I've been retained by Global Data Systems so I must be careful to uphold the attorney client privilege."

"Where you under contract with Global at the time you discussed the temporary assignment with Jackie Rogers?"

Sanders glanced over at Agent Hale. He now regretted the dramatic way he signed the contract in front of her. "No."

"Then any conversation you had before actually signing the contract could not possibly be subject to attorney client privilege, could it?"

"I suspect not."

"I can assure you I know the law. It does not apply to any such conversations." Agent Lee leaned back in his chair. "Will you now please tell us why you were retained to represent Global Data Systems instead of some high-powered attorney?"

Sanders sighed. "Well, Ms. Rogers said there was a conflicts problem with almost every law firm she contacted. Global Data Systems administers health plans for hundreds of large corporate clients nation-wide. All these plans retain outside law firms for legal counsel from time to time."

Agent Lee fiddled with his pen. "Okay, if that's what they told you. I still think it's odd that Global Data Systems would hire someone out of retirement." He paused and held his pen still. "Regardless, what kind of assignment were you hired to perform?"

"To conduct an independent investigation of improperly disclosed client health benefit information."

"I see. How many discussions with Ms. Rogers did you have prior to being retained by Global Data Systems?"

"Just the one call to set up the meeting and then only one meeting in person."

Agent Lee made a light scratch on his legal pad. Sanders suspected the agent was checking off the list of questions.

"During any of these discussions, were you given any possible leads as to who might be involved with the disclosures."

"No, I assumed that's why I was retained."

"Were you asked to sign any kind of non-disclosure agreement?"

Sanders groaned. "Yes, and I'm breaching it by speaking with you"

"So, I take it that the NDA is not restricting your answers today?"

"That's correct."

Agent Lee continued. "What else did you and Ms. Rogers discuss?

Sanders leaned forward. "We discussed the legal ramifications for improperly disclosing protected health information."

Agent Lee said, "Did you discuss the specific cases where information was disclosed?"

"Only in a general way. One case involved medical information related to someone's treatment for AIDS and another involved information related to a sexually transmittable disease."

Agent Lee jotted on his notepad. "So, you discussed just two cases?"

Sanders nodded. "Yes, we discussed only these cases prior to my being formally retained."

"What about subsequent to your being retained?"

Sanders cleared his throat. "Any such information would be subject to attorney client privilege."

Agent Lee said, "What else did you discuss with Jackie Rogers?"

"I asked if she thought of providing some incentives to employees who might come forward with any information relevant to the improper disclosures. She indicated she had not considered that idea."

"Did you discuss anything else?"

Sanders shifted in his seat. "Yes, I told Ms. Rogers some of the information I might believe to be useful in investigating. That would be workflow charts, organizational charts of the account where the improper disclosures occurred, and so forth."

"Account? So, only one Global Data Systems account was involved?"

"At the time of our conversation, that's correct."

Agent Lee tapped on his legal pad with his pen. "How long have you been on this temporary assignment?"

Sanders glanced upwards. "I just started Monday."

"How's your investigation progressing?"

Sanders twisted his mouth sideways. "I've really only scratched the surface."

Agent Lee rested his elbows on the table. "Any suspects emerge so far as to who the culprit or culprits might be?"

Sanders paused to ponder the question. He was

determined not to violate the attorney client privilege. "No, I don't have any suspects yet."

"Mr. Pierce, I want to remind you that the attorney client does not protect communications regarding criminal activity or the cover up of criminal activity by your client,"

Sanders nodded. "Yes, I'm aware of the crime-fraud exception to the privilege."

"If you do uncover criminal activity on the part of your client," Agent Hale said, "you're to contact me directly."

"Yes, Agent Hale. I suspect though if my investigation is successful, I will uncover some criminal activity on the part of an employee or two who are involved, instead of my client."

"If that turns out to be the case, you will contact me as well."

Sanders forced a smile. "Of course."

"I also need to remind you," Agent Lee said, "that, as far as the outside world is concerned, this deposition never occurred."

Sanders moaned. "That's not quite possible. I was with my next-door neighbor when I was served with the subpoena. In fact, I read it in her presence. She doesn't know the purpose of the deposition, but she knows I was to be deposed by the FBI."

"Is it correct to assume that this neighbor is not any way affiliated with Global Data Systems?"

"No, she's informed me that she's a therapist of sorts."

Agent Lee shifted in his chair to look down the table toward his colleagues. "Anything else I need to cover?"

Both shook their heads.

Agent Hale glanced over at the court reporter. "Thank you, I think that concludes the deposition."

The court reporter said, "Yes ma'am. I'll have the transcript ready tomorrow by the close of business. Shall I close the door behind me?"

Agent Hale smiled. "Yes, thank you."

That was the first time Sanders had seen her smile.

"By accepting this temporary assignment," Agent Hale said, "you may come across some things certain people may not want revealed."

Sanders smiled. "I suspect the culprit or culprits would definitely not want to be identified for their actions."

She squinted at Sanders. It was that same severe look she exhibited the first time he met her. "What I'm trying to delicately say is that you would be wise to proceed with caution."

"You make it sound like I'm walking into some kind of trap." He wrinkled his forehead. "Do you know something I don't?"

She shook her head. "We're at the preliminary stage of our investigation as well. However, we are trained to anticipate every type of scenario."

"Thank you for the warning. Do you need me for anything further?"

"No, I'll escort you down to the lobby."

Sanders sat in his Spider before starting the ignition. *I suspect Agent Hale knows more than she's willing to tell me.*

He turned the key. *Hell, I hope I didn't goof by agreeing to do this job!*

Chapter 11

After his deposition, Sanders decided to take Thursday afternoon off. He made the mistake of driving north on Interstate 35 when he left FBI headquarters. A wreck in the northbound lane just south of the Empire Central intersection forced traffic to slow down. Sanders exited at Mockingbird Lane and took a circuitous route back to his townhouse in Richardson. He arrived home at 2:00 p.m.

As was his custom, he exited his unit to check to see if he had any mail. When he reached his mailbox, he spotted his next-door neighbor pulling out of her driveway.

Claire lowered her window and said, "You're home a little early, aren't you, Sanders?"

"Yelp. I decided to take the afternoon off."

"How did your deposition go this morning?"

Sanders frowned. "About like I expected. Just a waste of time."

She gestured with her left hand. "I've got to run a couple of errands. Since you're home early, would you care to stop by for a glass of wine around 5:30?"

He smiled and nodded. "I'd love to. Do you like chardonnay?"

Claire's eyes lit up. "I love chardonnay."

"I've got a bottle of Ramey that I'll bring with me."
She smiled. "Perfect, see you at 5:30 p.m."
"I'll be over then."

* * *

Sanders decided to change into blue jeans and a sport shirt before heading next-door. *No corporate garb for me now.* He grabbed a bottle of Ramey Chardonnay from his refrigerator. Claire answered the door a few seconds after Sanders rang the doorbell.

He grinned. "That was fast. I guess your black yoga pants and matching top help make you quick."

"I was in my office downstairs and saw you pass by the window."

Sanders held up the bottle of Chardonnay. "I come bearing gifts."

She chuckled. "Excellent. Let's go upstairs and indulge."

They talked, laughed, and finished off the entire bottle of wine in just over two hours. Sanders glanced at his watch. "Oh my, it is 7:40 p.m., I'd better run and let you get on with your evening."

Claire patted his arm. "Do you have a busy day tomorrow?"

He groaned. "Yes, I want to get to Global Data Systems early and hit the ground running since I missed today."

"I know you can't discuss the specifics, but are

you finished with the FBI?

Sanders shrugged. "I can only hope so. But time will tell."

She said, "I'll see you out."

As they approached the edge of the stairs, Claire said, "Hey, would you like to see my playroom?"

He raised an eyebrow. "This is where you conduct your therapy, right?"

She winked at him. "Yes. I hope you're not freaked out."

His eyes widened. "Do you think I might be?"

Claire waved her right hand toward the hall. "Follow me this way."

Since Sanders' unit was the mirror image of hers, he already knew the exact layout. The master bedroom was to the left and the smaller guest room was straight ahead at the end of the hall. When they reached the landing at the top of the stairs on the third floor, both bedroom doors were closed.

Claire flipped on the overhead light. She walked down the short hall and grabbed the handle of the doorknob to the guest bedroom. Cracking the door just a bit, she switched on the overhead light in the bedroom. A red glow filtered out of the gap between the door and the frame.

Claire spun around to face Sanders and grinned. "Brace yourself." She pushed the door wide open behind her. "Let me show you around."

They both entered the room and Claire shut the door. After a few seconds, Sanders' eyes adjusted to the low-level red lighting. A long table with straps was positioned in the middle of the room. In one corner was a large chair. In the other corner was a large structure in the shape of the letter "X".

Claire walked to the left side of the room where several leather and plastic devices hung in a row. Facing Sanders, she ran her right hand down the first row. "These are my various whips, crops, wands, and paddles."

She took a few more steps toward the end of the wall. "These are my collections of gags, collars, and miscellaneous restraint tools." She jerked her thumb at one corner of the room. "That's my throne."

Sanders' mouth had dropped open long ago.

Claire pointed to the other corner of the room. "That large hunk of wood is my St. Andrew's Cross."

"What's that used for?" Sanders' croaked.

She chuckled. "Restraint and control."

He walked over to the St. Andrew's Cross to get a closer look. Thick leather straps and buckles were attached to each end of the cross. "You restrain your clients by their feet and hands?"

She nodded. "If the situation calls for it."

Sanders turned around and pointed at a long narrow padded table in the middle of the room next to where Claire stood. "Judging by the straps dangling off the edge, I assume that table is also used for restraint?"

Claire patted the table with her right hand. "Yes, that and bondage."

He narrowed his eyes. "You call what you do a form of psychotherapy?"

She grinned. "Yes. Most definitely."

Claire gestured to two chairs facing each other against the right wall. The only two normal pieces of furniture in the whole room. "Why don't we sit and talk? I can see you're having trouble wrapping your brain about my work."

Sanders sat in the chair nearest the door and Claire sat in the other chair. "Fire away with your questions," she said.

He opened his mouth but paused before he continued. "Wouldn't you be better described as a dominatrix rather than a psychotherapist?"

She rubbed her chin. "I suppose, but in my mind, there's a clear distinction. When I think of domination involving a dominatrix, right or wrong, there's an element of sex involved. People seek the services of a dominatrix strictly to satisfy some sexual need they derive from pain or, in some cases, actual sex of some kind."

Sanders wrinkled his forehead. "Can't the same be said for the services you provide?"

Claire shook her head. "No. If someone seeks that, I inform him or her that we're not a good fit."

He leaned forward. "But, how can you be sure?"

"Vetting. The first couple of sessions I have with a potential client are in-depth discussions concerning his or her expectations. I have enough experience to assess whether someone is sincere in what they're seeking. Even if they're lying about the reasons they want to see me, I can figure them out pretty quickly."

"Have you ever been mistaken, only to discover during a session that someone is not here for the right reasons?"

She smirked. "Of course. On the few occasions that has occurred, the session is immediately terminated."

Sanders shifted in his chair. "In those instances, do the people just voluntarily leave?"

Claire reached down and knocked on the laminated wood floor. "So far, I've had no issues."

"Let me make sure I understand. Your clients are solely here for non-sexual reasons."

She nodded. "They're here to give up complete control for the duration of the session. That's the power exchange. It's very therapeutic to turn over every fiber of power to someone you trust, if just for an hour."

Sanders scratched his head. "That just seems very foreign to me."

Claire reached over and patted his knee. "You should try it sometime."

He smiled. "Perhaps I will someday. But for now, I need to go home."

She stood up. "I'll walk you down."

Before they exited the room, Sanders laughed out loud.

"What's so funny?"

"It just occurred to me that your playroom is right next to my bedroom. I never in a thousand years would have imagined what was just a few inches of sheetrock away from where I sleep."

Claire laughed. "Well, now you have something to think about to help you sleep at night."

When they reached the front door, Claire said, "Hang on just a second."

Sanders stopped and turned around. Claire disappeared into the small first floor study and returned a few seconds later. She held a key up. "I'm going out of town for a few days. Would you mind keeping watch on my place?"

She handed it to him. "Here's the key to my front door, should you need to get into my house for any reason."

He grasped the key. "Sure, I promise though to stay out of your playroom."

"Of course." Claire laughed. "I bet you sneak up there the minute I leave." She gave him a quick peck on the cheek. "Good night, neighbor."

Sanders smiled. "Good night."

He made the short trek back to his unit and went upstairs to the second floor living area. He plopped into his Eames lounger.

Oh my, I wasn't expecting Claire to be a dominatrix, nor did I expect to ever have feelings for her.

Chapter 12

Sanders arrived early Friday morning at Global Data Systems. He pulled up the health claims processing workflow chart for the Beta Account, wanting to make certain he interviewed the manager of every step in the workflow.

The Stevie Greene debacle had caused him to go down a rabbit hole and skip the step before, which was Decryption of Images and Records. The Beta organization chart listed Janet Stewart as Interim Manager.

Sanders emailed the gatekeeper for Beta and requested an interview with Janet Stewart. The gatekeeper responded in under ten minutes, indicating Ms. Stewart would be available at 9:00 a.m. That gave him enough time to review his notes from the beginning of his investigation.

At 8:59 a.m., two knocks came on his office door. He walked over to the door and opened it. A woman in her late twenties dressed in a light gray pantsuit and white blouse was standing outside. Her long walnut brown hair was pulled back into a ponytail. She extended her hand. "Mr. Pierce, I'm Janet Stewart."

Sanders stepped to the side. "Please come in, Janet, and have a seat."

She slid into the client chair nearest the door. Sanders closed the door and made his way back to his office chair. He plopped down and picked up his pen.

"First of all, thank you for coming on such short notice."

"Uh, sure."

Sanders picked up the organization chart. "I see you're listed as the Interim Manager."

Janet nodded. "Yes, I've only been in the position about three weeks. I'm still trying to learn all aspects of the job."

He narrowed his eyes. "Why the 'interim' title?"

She shrugged. "I assume management is trying to determine if I can do the job before I'm made permanent."

"That makes sense. Were you an assistant manager in the Decryption area?"

Janet shook her head. "No, I was in another department altogether."

"May I ask what department?"

Janet ran her hand over the side of her head, then swished her ponytail. "I was an assistant manager in Global Data Systems Retirement Benefits."

Sanders raised an eyebrow. "Really? Why do you think they picked you as Interim Director for this position then?"

"I'm not certain. Although it's common for Global Data System employees to be moved around so that they can gain experience." She shrugged and stared at the floor.

He jotted some notes on his legal pad. "What happened to your predecessor in the Decryption area?"

Janet sighed. "He passed away."

"I'm sorry. Was he an elderly man?"

She shook her head. "I didn't know him personally, but I believe he was in his thirties. Someone assaulted him in his driveway. He was dead on arrival at the hospital."

Sanders straightened up in his chair. "That's horrific. Did the police catch whoever attacked him?"

"No," Janet said with a groan, "but the police were on campus interviewing everyone in his department for possible suspects."

Sanders raised an eyebrow. "What about the FBI?"

"I'm not aware whether they were involved or not... but I suppose they might have been."

"What was the manager's name?"

"Richard Rice."

Sanders jotted on his legal pad. "Janet, who directly reports to you in your current position?"

She rubbed her chin. "I have three direct reports. Jennifer Doak, my administrative assistant, John Stafford, Supervisor of Processing, and Mary Teague, Quality Control Supervisor."

Sanders shifted in his chair. "Were all three of them working in the Decryption area during your predecessor's tenure?"

Janet shook her head. "No, my administrative assistant came over to the area with me. John and Mary were already here, though."

Sanders scratched more notes on his legal pad. "Janet, who would you say is the most knowledgeable person in the Decryption area. By that I mean, is there someone who knows all the nuances of how the area works?"

She wrinkled her forehead. "Let's see. I'm not sure anyone currently fits that description. That's supposed to be my role, but I'm not there yet."

Sanders stared down at his legal pad and sighed. "I think that's all the questions I have for you. Thank you for your time."

As soon as Janet left his office, Sanders sent an email to the gatekeeper, requesting an interview with John Stafford.

* * *

Friday afternoon at 2:00 p.m., John Stafford knocked on Sanders' office door. Sanders crossed the room and opened the door. John was a short rotund man with a thick mane of blond hair, red face, wearing a navy-blue suit, white shirt, and red tie. Sanders could not help but notice that John's red tie was a perfect match for the red in his face.

So much for corporate coordination.

John slid into one of the client chairs and right away crossed his short legs.

Sanders plopped into his office chair. "Thank you for meeting with me, John."

John did not answer. He gazed down at Sanders legal pad, wearing a solemn expression.

"As I understand, you're the Supervisor of Processing. Can you fill me in on what your job entails?"

John uncrossed his legs. "Yes, I oversee all the decrypted data that is entered into the two systems that then are sent to Batching of Records and Files area."

Sanders paused. He recalled that Fred Stiers, the Manager of Records and Files said the decrypted data was received into one system, not two.

Sanders narrowed his eyes. "Did you say the data is entered into two systems?"

"Yes, the same data is entered into two systems."

"Why not just one system?"

John shrugged. "Beats me. It's not my role to question anything after the data is entered."

Sanders did not know if he heard Fred Stiers wrong or if the second system was for safekeeping or some other business reason. Nonetheless, he made a note to revisit the issue with Fred.

Sanders looked up from his legal pad. "How many operators are under your supervision?"

"Sixteen."

Sanders arched an eyebrow. "As I understand, it only takes eight operators in Batching and Records to key the data received from your area. I wonder why that area needs only eight operators instead of sixteen. I would think it would take the same number in both areas."

John scratched his head. "Listen, I don't know anything about Batching and Records. There were sixteen operators when I got the supervisor job and I suspect there will be sixteen whenever I leave."

Sanders stared down at his legal pad. "I'm sure you know I've been retained to investigate the improper disclosure of private health information."

John nodded. "Of course."

Sanders leaned back in his chair. "Do you have any ideas how the information leaked out?"

John's face turned a deeper shade of red. "No, sir, I don't have a clue."

Sanders sighed. "Okay, John, that's all the questions I have for you."

John sprang to his feet and all but sprinted the short distance to the door.

* * *

Sanders scheduled one last interview before the weekend, Mary Teague, Quality Control Supervisor. At the designated time of 4:00 p.m., Sanders looked up from his notes when a knock came on his office door. He ambled over and opened it. "You must be Mary."

"Yes, that's me."

Mary was a tall thin woman. She had very pale

skin and chestnut brown hair pulled back into a bun.

Her dark suit and horn-rimmed glasses certainly nail the conservative corporate look.

Sanders said, "Please have a seat."

She slid into a client chair. "Will this take long? I must pick up my daughter at day care at 5:30 p.m."

Sanders sat down in his chair. "Hopefully, this will only take less than thirty minutes."

She sighed. "Great, thank you."

He leaned back in his chair. "Help me understand a bit about what you do."

Mary gripped the armrests of the chair until her knuckles turned pale, and it appeared to Sanders that she was uncomfortable.

"I oversee Quality Control. I analyze all stages of claims processing to see where we can improve in efficiency and quality."

"So, you must be familiar with all aspects of the services the Beta Account provides, correct?"

She nodded. "That's pretty accurate."

"If that's the case," Sanders said as he squinted at her, "then why do you report to the Manager of Decryption of Images and Records?"

She frowned. "That's the million dollar question. I don't know. It never made sense to me."

"How long have you been in this position?"

Mary fidgeted in her chair. "Almost nine months."

Sanders jotted on his legal pad. "So, you're fairly new to the position."

"That's correct."

"Is this your first position at Global Data Systems?"

She nodded. "Yes, I was previously with Hewlett-Packard in the same kind of position."

Sanders leaned forward. "I'm curious, do you see many differences in how both companies process claims?"

Mary adjusted her glasses. "There's a lot of similarities, but some differences as well. Each company has its own culture, which influences how things get done."

Sanders glanced at his legal pad. "One aspect of the decryption process puzzles me. John Stafford told me that all decrypted data is entered by his team of operators into two separate systems. Is that correct?"

Mary rolled her eyes. "Yes. One goes to Batching of Records."

Sanders wrinkled his forehead. "What about the other one?"

She shrugged. "I don't know."

"As the Supervisor of Quality Control, I would have thought you would know the destination of the data in the other system."

Mary's face muscles tightened. "I did question my prior manager about it. He was evasive in his answer but said it was for safekeeping purposes."

Sanders made a note on his legal pad. "Why do you say he was evasive?"

"First, he told me not worry about it. When I pressed him on it, he said it goes to safekeeping. I then asked if I could analyze the process for quality control purposes."

"What happened next?"

He told me only upper management could authorize my involvement. When I requested that he get management's approval, he said he would look into it. After a while, I just gave up on the issue."

Sanders shifted in his chair. "So, you were kept completely in the dark by your manager about the other system."

"That's correct."

"Let me ask, did Hewlett Packard have decrypted data entered two systems?"

Mary shook her head. "No, only one."

Sanders glanced at his watch. "I promised to get you out of here. Just one last question. Do you know who your prior manager reported to within Global Data Systems?"

"Yes, he and all the managers of the health care administration report to Dan Wooten, the Account Manager for Beta."

Sanders stood up. "Thank you, Mary. You've been very helpful."

After Mary left, Sanders spent thirty minutes writing detailed notes on all the day's activities.

I don't know if I'm going down another rabbit hole, but I want to find out if there is anything to this mysterious second system next week.

Preparing to leave, Sanders stacked his papers to pack up in his brief case when someone knocked on his door. He hurried across the room and opened it.

A large muscular man with a stern expression stood there, looking down at Sanders. He was dressed, same as everyone else, in a navy suit, white shirt, and navy tie.

In a booming deep voice, he said, "Sanders Pierce?"

Sanders stared up at him. "Yes, I'm Sanders."

"I'm Allan Collins, Head of Corporate Security. Jackie said you wanted to talk to me."

Sanders took a step back. "Yes Allan, please have a seat."

He slid his bulky frame into a client chair.

Sanders settled in behind the desk. "I just have a few questions to tie up some loose ends. As I understand, all the client health data received by the three health accounts is scanned and encrypted. Then the original documentation is sealed and placed in secured safekeeping under the control of Corporate Security, is that correct?"

Allan stared at Sanders without blinking. "That's accurate. The original data is placed in a vault safe."

Sanders shifted in his chair. "Who has access to this vault safe?"

"Myself and my direct reports in the department. The safe is programmed to require a minimum of two people to open it. It reads fingerprints. If it doesn't recognize an approved fingerprint, it won't open. Every time it's opened, both Jackie Rogers and I receive a text message that the safe is being accessed."

As he tilted his head to one side, Sanders eyes

widened. "That's pretty good security."

Allan nodded. "It's the state of the art. There are several security cameras in the area which record all activity outside and inside the safe."

Sanders rubbed his chin. "I'm convinced. I think you've tied up any possible loose ends I may have had. I appreciate your time."

Chapter 13

Sanders got up early Saturday morning. It was a cool cloudy day when he walked the short distance to the UT Dallas campus. He enjoyed jogging around the perimeter of soccer fields on the south side of campus.

After completing an invigorating run, Sanders walked a circuitous route home on a secluded paved pathway he had discovered a few weeks ago. Just east of the soccer fields, a border of tall pine trees ran south all the way down to Campbell Road. Seldom did he encounter anyone on the pathway, even on weekends when the soccer fields were alive with activity.

At a clearing in the trees about halfway down to Campbell Road, one could just barely make out the road that connected to the east entrance of the campus. Sanders guessed it must be a couple of football fields away.

As mist fell, the clouds darkened on the west horizon. Sanders jogged toward Campbell and then back to the gated community where he lived. He was determined to outrace what he thought was a fast-moving incoming storm.

When he turned onto the street which ran in front of his townhouse, the bottom dropped out of the sky.

Sanders sped up and managed to miss the worst of the rain by mere seconds.

As he passed his next-door neighbor's unit, he spotted a large package on her front porch. Sanders remembered that Claire was going out of town. Once inside his own place, he opened his desk drawer and fished out the key to her unit.

The rain tapered off for a few seconds, giving him just enough time to sprint the few yards from his porch to her porch. He unlocked her front door and slid the long package into her entry hall. When he opened the door to leave, he flinched and almost dropped the key.

A young man in a dark jogging suit, runners, and black cap pulled down over his face was standing on the porch just outside the door. "Is Claire here?" he said in a clipped tone.

"Uh... uh, no... She... she's out of town."

"Who are you?"

"I'm her neighbor." Sanders turned away from the man and re-locked Claire's front door as fast as he could turn the key.

"What are you doing in her place?" His tone turned gruff.

Rain fell harder. Sanders said, " I was putting a package inside that was left on her porch. I didn't want it to get wet. Who are you, anyway?"

"I had an appointment with Claire yesterday, but she left a voice mail cancelling it. I was hoping she was here today."

Sanders wrinkled his forehead. "Well, she's not here."

The man sighed. "Okay, man, do you know when she'll be back?"

Sanders shook his head. "No, she didn't say."

The man glanced over his shoulder and then turned to run south down Grove Park Lane. He opened the door to a silver Acura MDX SUV that was parallel parked on the opposite side of the street and slid into the driver's seat. Sanders watched as the man eased the SUV out of a tight parking place and sped away.

What a strange encounter. I guess Claire has all types of clients! He drives a nice car, though.

* * *

Saturday afternoon, Sanders decided to stop by his gallery to check on things. He had not been there since he began his temporary assignment with Global Data Systems. He pulled into the small parking lot in front of the gallery and parked the Spider next to Taylor's red Honda Accord.

She must have spotted him on the security camera because she opened the front door to the gallery before he reached it. "Hey, Sanders, I didn't expect to see you today."

He chuckled. "I just thought I would drop by to check on you and make sure you haven't quit."

Taylor laughed. "No, I'm still gainfully employed."

He closed the door behind him. "How's everything going?"

"Pretty good. We've had a couple of visitors today. The good news though is that I sold one of your pieces last Wednesday."

His eyes widened. "Really, which one?"

She whirled around and pointed at the empty spot on the right wall. *Downpour*. I haven't replaced it on the wall yet."

"Fantastic. That should pay the bills another week."

Taylor wrinkled her forehead. "By the way, a woman stopped by yesterday afternoon and asked about you."

"Really?" He jerked his head toward the office. "Let's go in there so we can talk."

After following him through the office door, by habit, Taylor slid into one of the client chairs.

"No, I'll sit there," Sanders said."You sit behind the desk. You're in charge while I'm on this assignment."

She jumped up. "Whatever you say."

He waited for her to get settled in his chair. "So, tell me about this woman."

Taylor rested her elbows on the top of the desk. "She came in around 4:00 p.m. I spotted her on the security monitor getting out of her car, so I met her at the front door. I invited her into the gallery and asked if there was anything I could help her with. While her eyes swept around the gallery, she inquired if you were here."

"Do you think she was interested in my art?"

Taylor shook her head. " No, I don't think so. She wanted to know if you would be in the gallery later today. Of course, I told her I didn't know your schedule. Then this is when she got creepy. She asked for your home address."

Sanders raised an eyebrow. "How did you respond?"

Taylor snickered. "I played dumb and said I didn't know and that I was temporary. The woman then sneered at me a few seconds. I think she was trying to intimidate me."

Sanders smiled. "What an idiot, if she thought she was going to intimidate you."

"I guess she figured that out, because she turned around and hurried out of the gallery."

Sanders rubbed his chin. "Do you think this person could be with the FBI?"

Taylor leaned back in her chair. "Nope, she was dressed in blue jeans and a sport jacket. She had her hair pulled back in a ponytail. That's not how I picture any FBI agent looking."

"You're probably right, unless she was undercover. Anyway, enough about this woman. How are things with you?"

She frowned. "I got rejected on another job opportunity."

His face softened. "I'm sorry, Taylor. Something good will turn up soon."

Sanders' telephone buzzed in his sport coat pocket.

He fished it out and at once felt tense. "Hello."

"Mr. Pierce."

"Yes." Sanders stood up.

"This is Agent Hale. Do you have a moment to speak?"

"Of course, agent."

Taylor's eyes widened as she listened to his end of the conversation.

"Are you at your home?"

"No, I'm at my art gallery."

"I need to meet with you. How long are you going to be there?"

"I'm not sure. I can be here as long as needed."

"Good. I'll be there in thirty minutes."

He rubbed the crown of his bald head. "Can you tell me what this is about?"

"I'd rather speak to you in person."

Sanders sighed. "Okay, Agent Hale. I'll wait for you."

Agent Hale hung up without responding.

He groaned and slipped the phone back in his coat pocket.

Taylor narrowed her eyes. "Everything okay?"

"I don't know. Agent Hale just said she needs to meet with me. So, she's coming here in about thirty minutes."

"That's the severe looking woman, isn't it?"

He nodded and started to tell Taylor about the deposition but caught himself as he recalled the specific order in the subpoena not to disclose anything about the nature of the deposition.

Taylor glanced at her phone. "I know it's a tad early, but would you like a glass of wine?"

He chuckled. "You're reading my mind."

They both walked back into the gallery over to the bar.

She said, "I'll get the glasses." Taylor pulled a bottle of Sonoma Cutrer Chardonnay out of the small refrigerator behind the bar and poured two glasses of wine. "I just opened this bottle yesterday when someone stopped by to check out the art. So, I know it's still good."

"Perfect, thanks."

Taylor slid in a seat next to him at the bar. "Do you have any idea what she wants to talk to you about?"

Sanders took a drink of wine. "I'm sure it has to do with Global Data Systems. But I have no idea the purpose of the meeting."

She twirled her wine around in the glass. "Do you want me to leave before she gets here?"

He shook his head. "That's not necessary. Just take off at your normal time."

Taylor finished off her glass of wine. "I'm going to go work on the press release for the next opening, unless you need to be in the office."

"No, that's fine. I'll go wait in my studio until Agent Hale arrives.

At precisely thirty minutes after Sanders' phone conversation with Agent Hale, Taylor appeared at the entrance to his studio. "Your date's here. I just saw her pull up in the parking lot."

Sanders laughed. " 'My date', you say. Well, I think I'll go greet her."

As he was making his way to the front of the gallery, he spotted Agent Hale through the window in the front of the gallery. She wore a white blouse, charcoal gray suit, and black pumps, and carried a black handbag.

Gosh, she'd fit in fine at Global Data Systems.

Sanders met her at the doorway. "Hello Agent Hale."

She scanned the interior of the gallery. "Mr. Pierce."

He motioned with his right hand. "Let's go to my studio. We can talk there."

She twisted her mouth into a half smile. "Lead the way."

As they entered the studio, Agent Hale said, "So, this is where you hang out when you're not taking temporary legal assignments."

Sanders nodded. "Yes, I can assure you. It's a lot more enjoyable to paint than to practice law of any kind. Please have a seat on the sofa."

She sat right in the middle of the sofa, so Sanders plopped down in the chair he uses while painting. Agent Hale pulled a notepad and pen out of her handbag and opened the notepad. She studied it a few seconds, then said, "Do you recall after your deposition that I told you to proceed with caution while you're on this temporary assignment with Global

Data Systems?"

"Yes, I recall you saying something to that effect."

Her eyes were laser focused on Sanders. "Are you aware that one of the managers in the Beta Account at Global Data Systems was a victim of homicide?"

He paused to consider the attorney client privilege ramifications. "Yes."

"May I ask how you learned about this incident?"

He sighed. "In the context of my investigation at Global Data Systems."

Her eyes widened. "That's good."

He wrinkled his forehead. "Why do you say 'that's good'?"

She leaned forward. "Because you should be hyper-cautious while you're on this assignment. The FBI is working with the Plano Police Department on investigating the homicide. One of the scenarios we're exploring for motive is that this guy was eliminated as a precaution."

Sanders shifted in his chair. "Precaution. What do you mean?"

Agent Hale exhaled. "We think his death may be linked to the illegal disclosure of health information by someone in the Beta Account. He either was directly involved in one or more of the leaks or knew something or someone who was involved."

He raised an eyebrow. "But couldn't the homicide be completely unrelated to Global Data Systems? Unless you know something else you're not telling me right now, that seems like a quantum leap to tie the two together."

"We've received some information from an anonymous source that corroborates the connection."

Sanders straightened up in his chair. "Do you think the source is credible?"

She nodded. "We have to assume the source is credible until the evidence leads elsewhere."

"That makes sense."

Agent Hale glanced down at her notepad. "Has anyone threatened you or have you observed anyone behaving in a suspicious manner since you've been on this assignment. When I say suspicious, have you spotted anyone hanging out by your car or near your house?"

Sanders shook his head. "No one has threatened me, and I haven't observed anyone suspicious hanging around my car or—"

He stopped when he remembered what Taylor had told him. "Taylor, who assists me here, said a woman inquired about me just yesterday."

She narrowed her eyes. "Is Taylor here?"

He nodded. "Shall I go get her?"

"Yes, please."

Sanders walked down the hallway to the office. He stuck his head in the door. "Agent Hale would like to speak to you."

Taylor's eyebrows shot up. "Why me?"

"It's about the person who came in yesterday and inquired about me."

She leapt to her feet. "Oh, okay."

When Taylor entered the studio, Agent Hale stood up and moved to the end of the sofa. "You must be Taylor." She patted the cushion next to her. "Please have a seat on the sofa."

Taylor did as she requested. Sanders plopped back down in his chair.

Agent Hale said, "Taylor, what's your last name?"

"Miller."

Agent Hale jotted on her notepad. "I understand that a woman came in yesterday and inquired about Mr. Pierce."

"Yes, the woman asked if Sanders was here. When she heard he wasn't, she wanted to know when he was coming in. I told her I didn't have his schedule. That's when it became weird. She wanted to know Sanders' home address. I played dumb and said I didn't know."

"Did she ask any other questions?"

Taylor shook her head. "No, she glared at me and stormed out of the gallery."

"What did this woman look like?"

"She was Caucasian. I'm guessing in her late twenties or early thirties. Her physique was quite buffed."

Agent Hale wrote in her notebook. Without looking up, she said, "What color were her eyes and hair?"

"She had dark brown, almost black, hair. I don't remember the color of her eyes to be totally honest."

"How was she dressed?"

Taylor glanced up at the ceiling as if that would help her remember the woman's clothing. "She was wearing a dark sport coat and I believe blue jeans and a light blue shirt."

Agent Hale gestured with her head in the direction of the parking lot. "Did you get a look at what kind of motor vehicle she was driving?"

Taylor shook her head. "Not really. I think it was some sort of dark colored sedan."

Agent Hale glanced over at Sanders. "Do you have any video from your security camera out front?"

Sanders moaned. "I used to keep the video recordings, but I stopped doing that a few months ago."

Agent Hale grimaced. "Is it possible to start taping again?"

He nodded. "Yes, I will activate it this afternoon."

Agent Hale turned her head to look at Taylor. "Thank you, Taylor. That's all we need from you."

Agent Hale waited until Taylor exited the studio, then said, "I know you have your attorney client privilege concerns, but please keep in mind the distinct possibility that the manager's homicide may be connected to the very thing you are investigating. If you see anything that corroborates that connection, I need you to immediately contact me."

Sanders swallowed hard. "Yes, Agent Hale. I'll do what I legally can do to help the FBI."

She studied her notebook for a few seconds. "I believe that's all we need to discuss. Any questions for me?"

"No, but thank you for giving me a heads up."

Agent Hale slipped the notebook inside her handbag and stood up. "Remember to activate your recording on your security cameras."

He sprung to his feet. "I'll do it right after you leave."

* * *

Before leaving the gallery for the evening, Sanders peered out the window and stared at his FIAT Spider.

Just over year ago, someone placed a bomb in my car, nearly killing me. If I hadn't returned inside the gallery to retrieve my phone, I would've been blown to smithereens.

He bit his lip. *I hope to hell, history isn't going to repeat itself!*

Chapter 14

The Monday morning commute to Global Data Systems took longer than usual. A brief downpour of rain had snarled traffic on the North Dallas Tollway. Sanders was relieved to find a space in Visitor Parking.

As soon as he reached his office, he opened his email. An email from Jackie Rogers requested a meeting in his office at 4:00 p.m.

The only other email to catch his eye was from the mysterious Emma Peel. He double checked to make sure it was from the same EmmaPeel22gmail.com who sent the prior email. Sanders opened the email.

> They're going to try and hide the ball from you!
> Emma

He decided to send an email to Emma Peel to see if she would respond.

> Emma,
> Thank you for the information. Can you tell me who they are and any other information that might assist in my investigation?

Sanders

I wonder what 'hiding the ball' means and who's Emma Peel?

Sanders checked his notes from last Friday to see if he could get a meeting with Dan Wooten, the Account Manager of Beta. He emailed a meeting request to the designated gatekeeper, then received an immediate response indicating that Dan Wooten was out of town and unavailable.

Sanders plotted his next move. Should he continue focusing his investigation on the Beta Account or switch gears and start investigating the Gamma Account where another breach occurred? Sanders wanted some closure to the Decryption issue before focusing on other areas of the claims process.

He pulled up and printed off the Gamma Account Organization Chart. The Manager of Decryption of Images was George Atkins. Sanders sent an email to the gatekeeper on the Gamma Account and requested a meeting with the manager.

The gatekeeper got back to him within thirty minutes and indicated that George Atkins would be able to meet with Sanders at 10:00 a.m. Sanders went through the organization chart to familiarize himself with the names. He then accessed the Gamma work-flow for claims processing. It was identical to the Beta Account in this perspective.

He checked the time at the bottom right of his computer screen. It was 9:55 a.m. He had a few minutes to sneak a peek at his email to see if Emma Peel had responded.

The only new email was from the gatekeeper confirming the 10:00 a.m. appointment. Someone knocked on his office door at 9:55. a.m. He strolled over and swung open the door. "You must be George Atkins."

"Yes, I'm Atkins." He was tall slender man wearing thick glasses and dressed in the corporate uniform of white shirt, dark suit, and bland gray tie. His thinning brown hair was slicked back above his shiny forehead.

Sanders could not help but think that George resembled the actor, Joe Turkel, in character as Dr. Eldon Tyrell in the 1980s movie *Blade Runner*. He motioned toward his client chairs. "Thank you, George, for coming on short notice. Please have a seat."

Both men got situated in their chairs and Sanders picked up the Gamma Organizational Chart more for show than anything. "I see you're the Manager of Decryption of Images and Records."

George's face had a blank expression. "Yes."

"Can you give me a description of your duties as the manager?"

George frowned. "Haven't you already questioned the manager in Beta about her duties? What makes you think my duties would be any different than hers?"

Sanders felt like he was back in court, questioning

a hostile witness. However, he didn't want to appear threatening. "That's correct, George. Can you tell me how long you've been in this position?"

"Two years."

Sanders feigned a smile. "As you probably know, Janet Stewart is relatively new to the position. Since you have more experience, I thought perhaps you might be better able to describe the duties required to be manager."

George crossed his legs and folded his arms, exhibiting the body language of someone who was uncomfortable answering the question. "It's pretty straight forward. The manager is responsible for making sure all images and records received from the server are decrypted and transferred over to the Batching area."

Sanders leaned back in his chair. "As I understand from the claims processing workflow, the encrypted records and images are stored in a secure server and then at the appropriate time transferred over to your area from decryption. Is that a fair description?"

"That's a bit simplistic but accurate description of the process."

"How does Decryption area receive the data?"

George pursed his lips. "Through the system. That's the only way it can be transferred."

Sanders narrowed his eyes. "By your answer, I assume there is only one system that feeds your area all the records and images, correct?"

George fidgeted in his chair. Sanders got a sense

that George knew where this line of questioning was heading. After a few moments, he said, "Yes."

"So, after you decrypt the records and images. I assume then you have them entered into one system for transfer to the Batching area. Would that be an accurate description?"

George sighed. "Actually, they're keyed into two systems."

Sanders picked up the Gamma workflow for claims processing and held it up so George could see it. He pointed at the arrow linking Decryption of Images and Records to Batching of Images and Files. Under the arrow was the word 'system'.

"Why isn't the word 'systems' used here instead of 'system'?"

George was shaking. "Be... because only one... one system ... transfers the images and records to Batching."

Sanders released the Gamma workflow for claims processing, and it floated back down to his desk. At last, he was able to ask the crucial question. "Well, if that's the case, why does the Decryption area enter the data into two systems, if only one system feeds Batching?"

George stared at the floor. "I'm told the other system goes to safekeeping."

Sanders raised one eyebrow. "Is it fair to say you don't know where the data goes in the other system?"

"Listen, that's not part of my job."

Sanders jotted on his legal pad. "Have you ever

inquired of your manager where that data goes?"

He shook his head but remained silent.

"George, who directly reports to you?"

George sighed. "My administrative assistant, Shirley Sargent, and the Supervisor of Processing, Rob David."

Sanders' eyes widened. "And what about the Supervisor for Quality Control?"

"No, she reports to the Account Manager."

"What's her name?"

"Debra Brannon."

Sanders stared down at his legal pad. "I think that's all the questions I have for you."

Sanders watched as George exited his office. He leaned back in his chair and closed his eyes.

There's something suspicious with that second system of decrypted data. But is it really for safekeeping purposes or is it somehow tied to the leaks of private medical information?

He crossed his arms behind his head and looked up at the ceiling. *Something or someone certainly has George Atkins spooked!*

* * *

At 4:15 p.m., a light knock came on his door. Before he could get out of his chair, Jackie Rogers opened the door. "Sorry, I'm late." She shut the door and plopped down in a client chair and shook her head.

Sanders said, "Everything okay?"

She sighed. "Just more issues to deal with."

He leaned forward. "Any more reports of private health care leaks?"

"Not that we're aware of anyway."

"You know, the leaks could turn out to be just a few isolated occurrences."

Jackie pursed her lips. "You don't really think that's the case, do you?"

He glanced at his legal pad full of page after page of notes. "No, I think the three cases are the tip of the iceberg."

"How's the investigation going?"

"I may very well be going down another rabbit hole, but I think I'm onto something."

Her eyes widened. "What have you found?"

Sanders held up the Gamma health claims processing workflow chart. The same as with George Atkins, he pointed at the arrow from Decryption to Batching. "There is only one system identified transporting the decrypted data leaving Decryption."

Jackie leaned forward and squinted at the workflow chart. "Why is that significant?"

"Do you see any other arrows transporting data from Decryption?"

She shook her head. "No."

Sanders set the workflow chart back down on his desk. "Well, in both Gamma and Beta, the identical decrypted data is entered into two systems. However, the workflow chart only shows one system. Employees I interviewed in both accounts said that the second system was for safekeeping."

Jackie shifted in her chair. "That would seem to make sense."

He rubbed his bald head. "Perhaps. But I'm a little suspicious that the second system may not be used solely for safekeeping."

"Why?"

"First, the Supervisor of Quality Control in Beta reports directly to Janet Stewart, the Manager of Decryption. Janet is new on the job and still finding her way around. As I'm sure you're aware, her predecessor was a homicide victim."

Sanders considered telling Jackie about Agent Hale's suggestion that his death and the leaked health information may be connected but remembered he was directed not to disclose the FBI involvement.

She wrinkled her forehead. "Yes, but what does that have to do with your investigation?"

Sanders flipped through his legal pad. "I interviewed Janet, John Stafford, Supervisor of Processing, and Mary Teague, Quality Control Supervisor. None of them seemed to be certain that the second system was used for safekeeping.:

He held up one finger. "What's more compelling is that the Quality Control Supervisor should report to the Account Manager since she's responsible for quality control for all of Beta. Instead, she reports to a new lower-level manager."

He switched to two fingers. "Second, Janet's deceased predecessor kept her in the dark about the second system. When she requested access to review all aspects of the second system, her manager thwarted all her attempts. He said approval would have to come from upper management, which apparently he never sought. At least, that's Mary's perspective on the matter. He just indicated the second system was used for safekeeping purposes."

Jackie grimaced. "I'm not sure that's really a red flag."

Sanders scanned his notes. "There's more. I just interviewed this morning George Atkins, Gamma's Manager of Decryption of Records and Images. He was visibly uncomfortable talking about the purpose of the second system. He indicated it was his understanding that the second system was for safekeeping purposes. He admitted he was not certain it was used for that purpose."

She sighed. "I'm still not convinced there's anything out of the ordinary here."

"Another unusual thing is that in the Gamma Account, the Supervisor of Quality Control reports to the Account Manager and not to George Atkins. He's been on the job much longer than Janet in Beta. Why wouldn't the two accounts be handled the same way?"

Jackie shrugged. "I don't know. Anyway, what's your next move?"

Sanders glanced at the Gamma Organizational Chart. "I want to talk with the Account Manager for Gamma, which according to the chart is Monty

Stevens. I tried to interview the Account Manager for Beta and was informed that he was out of town and unavailable."

Jackie straightened up in her seat. "That makes sense."

"Jackie, do you know either one of these managers?"

She shook her head. "I may have met them on some occasion, but I really don't recall." She glanced at her watch. "I need to get back upstairs. Anything else we need to discuss?"

He leaned back in his chair. "There's one last thing.

What's that?"

"I received two quite interesting emails from EmmaPeel@sbcglobal.net."

Jackie cocked her head. "Why is that name familiar?"

Sanders chuckled. "Remember Diana Rigg played the part of Emma Peel in the 1960 TV series, *The Avengers*?"

She rolled her eyes. "Yes, of course. What were the nature of these emails?"

He shrugged. "The first simply said something to the effect that things are not always as they seem and a second one stated they're going to 'try and hide the ball'."

"While the emails sound nefarious, they also sound like someone is trying to prank you." Jackie stood up. "Listen, I have to run. Let me know if anything else develops."

"Will do."

Before Sanders called it a day, he sent the Gamma gatekeeper an email requesting a meeting with Monty Stevens, the Account Manager for Gamma.

Chapter 15

Sanders got up extra early on weekdays so he could get his exercise before work. Tuesday morning was cool as dawn was breaking. It took him just over ten minutes to reach the soccer fields on the UT Dallas campus. He jogged clockwise around the fields before stopping for a drink of water from a fountain on the east side of the fields. It was cloudy and overcast.

He considered taking a more direct route back home but decided to go ahead and take the pathway south to Campbell Road. As usual, he met no one on the pathway.

It was extra dark with the cluster of tall pine trees surrounding both sides of the pathway shielded what little sunlight that managed to filter through the clouds. After ten minutes he reached a part of the pathway where there was a ten-yard clearing on the east side. During a clear day, the road leading from the east campus entrance to the center of campus was just visible on the east horizon.

Midway through the clearing, his right shoelace came untied. He was in the process of dropping to one knee to tie his shoe, when something that made a shrill crack flew over his head and smashed into the trunk of pine tree on the west side of trail. The crash sparked and ripped the bark of the tree open upon impact.

Sanders lost his balance and fell face first on the concrete pathway. He froze in position, trying to grasp what he just experienced. A few seconds passed before he pushed himself up to a kneeling position. He scanned the east horizon and spotted a black car speeding south towards the east entrance to campus.

What the hell just happened?

He managed to get to his feet. His left elbow was stinging where it had scraped the concrete. Sanders ambled over and examined the tree, finding a two-inch wound on the trunk where an object struck it. A sudden chill shot down his spine.

I think someone just took a shot at me.

Sanders' stomach recoiled, making him a bit unsteady on his feet. His heart pounded in his chest.

Instead of continuing down the pathway south, he turned around and jogged north on the pathway, back to where he started. If the shooter was driving the black car, Sanders did not want to go anywhere near Campbell Road.

He stopped to catch his breath when he reached the top of the pathway where the sightlines were clear. Except for a woman jogging around the perimeter of the soccer fields, no one was there. Sanders continued jogging until he reached his townhouse. He unlocked the front door, dashed several steps into

his entry hall, and bent over at the waist, panting.
Should I call the FBI?

* * *

Sanders arrived a little bit late to Global Data Systems. He parked his Spider as close to the entrance as possible. When he exited his car, he stood and surveyed the entire parking lot before hurrying up the sidewalk to the entrance.

He breathed a sigh of relief as he entered the building. As soon as he got situated in his office, he pulled up his email. The first message was from the Gamma gatekeeper concerning his request for a meeting with Monty Stevens, the Gamma Account Manager. The same as with the Beta Account, the gatekeeper indicated Monty Stevens was out of town and unavailable.

Sanders wondered if the two account managers were really out of town. He picked up the Gamma Organization Chart. He fired off an email to the Gamma gatekeeper and requested an interview with Sarah Silvers, administrative assistant to Monty Stevens.

If she's not available. I may have to push back!

He scrolled through the remainder of his unread emails. He pulled up an email from EmmaPeel22A@ gmail.com. It read:

I must be very guarded with the content of

the emails I send you. I do not want to be
identified. It is possible your emails are
being monitored.

Sanders stared at his computer screen. It had
already occurred to him that perhaps his emails
were monitored.

An email popped up on the screen. The Gamma
gatekeeper responded that Sarah Silvers was not
available. She was tied up with matter of extreme
importance for Mr. Stevens.

Sanders groaned. He pulled up the Beta
Organization Chart and sent an email to the Beta
gatekeeper, requesting an interview with Lisa Hall,
the administrative assistant to the Beta Account
Manager. If she's not available, Sanders was going
to fire off an email to Jackie Rogers.

He was a bit surprised he was able to get an
interview with Lisa at 2:00 p.m. That afternoon,
Sanders left his office door open.

At 2:10 p.m., Lisa Hall, a tall willowy blond
woman, wearing a white blouse and blue pantsuit,
carrying a notepad and pen, stuck her head in the
doorway. "Mr. Pierce, I'm Lisa Hall." She waited in
the doorway.

Sanders gestured toward his client chairs.
"Please have a seat, Lisa."

She closed the door and strode over and eased
into the chair nearest the door. "I assumed you
wanted me to shut the door."

"Sure, thank you." He leaned forward. "First, thank you for meeting with me on short notice."

Lisa smiled. "Of course."

"As I understand, you're the administrative assistant to the Account Manager of Beta."

She nodded. "Yes, that would be Dan Wooten."

"How long have you been in this position?"

"Almost two years."

Sanders jotted on his legal pad. "And were you employed by Global Data Systems prior to accepting this position?"

"Oh yes. I was employed here right after I finished college."

"My goodness. You probably know everything there is to know about Global Data Systems."

She chuckled. "Yes, I guess you could say that."

"I understand Dan Wooten is out of town."

Lisa rolled her eyes. "Technically, that's correct. He and the two other health account managers meet every other week offsite in Dallas."

Sanders narrowed his eyes. "Why would they need to meet offsite?"

"Dan said it was so they wouldn't be disturbed and could get more done."

"Do you think perhaps there's another reason they meet offsite?"

She shifted in her chair. "Dan's not the most trustworthy guy I've ever met. I take everything he says with a grain of salt."

Sanders wrinkled his forehead. "Why do you

continue to work for him then?"

Lisa sighed. "I'm paid very well, and my job is very secure. I know more than Dan about how to manage the Beta Account."

"If that's the case, it sounds to me like you should be the manager then."

She smiled. "I agree. Global Data Systems has one of thickest glass ceilings you could ever imagine."

Sanders leaned back in his chair. "Jackie Rogers is General Counsel. How did she manage to break through the glass ceiling?"

"Simple. She's from outside the corporation. If you start at Global Data Systems, different standards apply. Nine out of ten times, a male will get a promotion over an equally qualified female."

"Then why do you stay?"

Lisa grimaced. "As I said before, I'm paid very well."

Sanders picked up his pen. "Let's change gears here. With all your knowledge of the Beta Account, do you have any ideas how or why the private health information was leaked?"

Her face tightened. "I have some suspicions who might be behind it. But at this stage, they're only suspicions."

"Care to share your suspicions with me?"

Lisa stared at Sanders a few seconds. "I think someone is profiting off the leaks."

"Do you have any credible proof who that might be?"

"It wouldn't surprise me if Dan was somehow involved."

"Why Dan?"

She ran a hand through her hair. "Because he's the Account Manager, and as I said, he's a little shaky in the integrity department."

Sanders jotted on his legal pad. "Let us say for the sake of argument that Dan is involved. Why leak certain information and how would he profit off the leaks?"

Lisa shook her head. "I haven't figured that out yet."

Sanders studied his legal pad. "I think that's all the questions I have for you. Do you have anything else you would like to tell me?"

"No, not at this time."

After Lisa left his office, Sanders sent an email to Jackie Rogers, requesting a gatekeeper be established in the Delta Account. To his surprise, she responded right away, inquiring why he needed to interview anyone in that account since to date, there had been no leaks. He indicated he wanted to ascertain if the workflow mirrored that in the other accounts. Jackie acquiesced and directed her administrative assistant to contact Delta to establish a gatekeeper.

Sanders decided to spend the rest of the day reviewing his notes and strategizing his next move. His cell phone buzzed on the desk. He picked it up and frowned when he read the caller's name.

"Hello."

"Hello, Mr. Pierce. This is Agent Hale."

Sanders leaned back in his chair. "What can I do for you, agent?"

"I wanted to inform you that we've narrowed our field of suspects in the Rice homicide."

"That was the manager of the Beta Account Decryption, correct?"

"Yes, Richard Rice. We're not able yet to make a connection between the homicide and what Rice's job was at Global Data Systems. Is there anything you have uncovered in your investigation that might be relevant? I'm cognizant of your attorney client privilege concerns."

Sanders sighed. "I cannot say I have found anything relevant to that connection. However, something happened to me this morning that you should probably know."

"What is it?"

"I think someone took a shot at me when I was getting my morning exercise over at UT Dallas."

"What? And you didn't immediately call me?"

Sanders could envision her tightened face staring holes in the phone. "I was going to call you later today"

"Where are you now?"

"I'm at Global Data Systems."

"Can you leave now and meet me at your home?"

Sanders flipped his legal pad closed. "I can be there in about twenty minutes, depending upon what the traffic is like."

"Excellent. I'll meet you there. We should still have ample daylight to go to the location where the incident occurred."

* * *

Sanders eased the Spider around the corner on to Grove Park Lane. A dark green sleek Lexus RC was parked in the fire lane right in front of his townhouse. Agent Hale was sitting behind the wheel. As he drew closer, she rolled down her window and waved at him. Sanders pulled up alongside her car and rolled down his window.

"Park your car and hop in," she said. "I'll drive."

He parked his Spider at the end of his driveway and jogged back around to Agent Hale's Lexus. He jumped into the passenger seat. "Nice car, Agent Hale."

Staring straight ahead, she cracked a slight smile. "It gets me around. Where to?"

Sanders directed her to the parking lot on the UT Dallas campus nearest where the north side of the secluded pathway was located. They both took off at a brisk pace south down the pathway.

"It happened a couple of hundred yards down the pathway," Sanders said, "where there's a small clearing in the trees."

Agent Hale's eyes darted back and forth, taking in the surroundings. "And what time were you here this morning?"

"Early, just after daybreak. I jog around the soccer fields and then take this route home because it's secluded and peaceful."

When they arrived at the clearing, Sanders said, "Right here is where it happened."

Agent Hale pulled a pen and notepad out of her bag. "Give me all the specifics."

He pointed down at the pavement. "When I reached this point, I noticed one of my runners had become untied. As I knelt down to tie my shoe, I heard a shrill crack just above my head and then the impact of the bullet splitting the bark of that tree."

They walked over to the tree. Agent Hale examined the tree's wound and snapped a picture of it on her cell phone.

She walked around to the other side of the tree. "There's no exit wound. With any luck, the bullet is still lodged in the trunk. I'll send Forensics over tomorrow to see if it can be recovered. Did you see the shooter?"

Sanders pointed east. "No, but a black car sped away on that access road toward the east entrance of the campus."

Agent Hale turned to walk off the pathway towards the east. "Let's see if we can recover a casing."

It took them about ten minutes to walk more than a hundred yards across the uneven terrain over to the access road. Sanders and Agent Hale paced down the road several times to the east entrance of the campus. Dusk was settling in.

"I don't think they'll find anything," she said, "but I'll have Forensics comb the area tomorrow morning."

* * *

Agent Hale pulled up in front of Sanders' townhouse. "One more thing, Mr. Pierce. Don't go down that pathway until we catch this perpetrator. And stay away from any other secluded place by yourself for that matter."

Sanders opened the car door. "You have my word, Agent Hale."

As soon as he exited the car, he spotted Claire on her front porch, lounging against the railing.

She said, "Well, well, who's the hot chick?"

He smiled. "The hot chick is FBI Agent, Angie Hale."

Claire's mouth dropped open. "Driving that fancy car?"

"Yep."

"What were the two of you doing?"

He sighed. "Believe it or not, we drove over to UT Dallas to see the spot where I was shot at this morning."

She jerked upright. "Are you serious?"

Sanders nodded. "I'm afraid so." He filled her in

on the details. "Agent Hale believes the attempt on my life might be related to my temporary assignment with Global Data Systems."

Claire stepped off her porch and walked over and hugged Sanders. "I thought you might need that."

"I did, thank you. Would you care for a glass of wine?"

She shook her head. "I would love one, but unfortunately, I have a client coming this evening. Can I get a rain check?"

He chuckled. "Of course. I'm right next door. By the way, you saw the package I left in your foyer, right?"

Claire nodded. "Yes, I just got home earlier today. I was going to drop by and thank you later."

"As I was leaving your townhouse, one of your clients met me on the front porch."

She wrinkled her forehead. "I didn't have any appointments scheduled. Was it a man or a woman?"

"It was a man. I didn't get his name, though."

Claire frowned. "Some of these clients can be needy."

* * *

Sanders went to bed early. He lay in bed and thought about Claire. *Does she have a client in her playroom just inches of sheet rock from where my bed is situated?*

He drifted off to sleep.

Chapter 16

Wednesday morning, Sanders pulled up his Global Data Systems email. An email from Jackie Rogers' administrative assistant gave him the phone number and email address of the gatekeeper for the Delta Account.

Sanders fired off an email to the gatekeeper, expressing his interest in interviewing the Decryption Manager and the Supervisor of Quality Control. He had not even taken the time to pull up the Delta Organization Chart to know the names of the persons who held those positions.

The other email that caught his attention was from the mysterious Emma Peel.

> You are doing fine. Watch your back and aim higher.

I wonder if the 'watch your back' reference had anything to do with the attempt on my life. He shook his head. *I'm still not convinced that whoever shot at me was not just some random kook.*

Sanders accessed all the information he could find regarding the Delta Account, when his phone rang. He jumped, because he seldom used his landline in his office.

He picked up the receiver. "Hello."

"Mr. Pierce?"

"Yes, I'm Pierce. How may I help you?"

"I'm Bonnie Sutherland, the assigned gatekeeper for the Delta Account."

Sanders leaned back in his chair. "Yes."

"I have arranged for you to meet with Mr. Delman Jenkins at 2:00 p.m. He's the Manager of Decryption of Images and Records for Delta. However, there's currently no Supervisor of Quality Control."

He raised an eyebrow. "Why isn't there anyone in the position of Supervisor of Quality Control?"

"Uh, because the position is vacant."

Sanders thought he detected some nervousness in Bonnie's voice. "How long has it been vacant?"

"A long time."

"Can you be more specific? I mean, are we talking days, weeks, or more?"

A sigh came from the other end of the line. "It's been vacant for over a year?"

Sanders grabbed his pen and jotted on his legal pad. "Why hasn't the position been filled?"

"I'm sorry, sir. I don't know."

"Who does the Supervisor of Quality report to in Delta?"

"That'd be the Delta Account Manager, Preston Zimmerman."

Sanders eyes widened. "Interesting. Thank you for the information."

"Is there anything else, Mr. Pierce?"

"No, that's all, thank you."

He considered requesting an interview with Preston Zimmerman but decided to wait until after he met with Delman Jenkins. Besides, Lisa Hall, the administrative assistant for Dan Wooten, indicated that all three account managers were meeting offsite.

Delman Jenkins arrived ten minutes late for his scheduled meeting with Sanders. He was a tall thin man with short blond hair, wearing a light gray suit, black tie, and white shirt. Sanders guessed him to be in his mid-forties. This was the first man he interviewed who was not dressed in the "corporate" charcoal gray suit.

As soon as he entered Sanders' office, Delman said, "I don't understand why you're questioning me. There haven't been any leaks from Delta."

Sanders motioned to the client chairs. "Please have a seat, Delman."

Delman plopped down in one of the client chairs. Sanders could tell Delman was perturbed due to his body language and frown.

"I'm cognizant of what you're saying. I just need to verify a few things. This shouldn't take too long."

Delman did not change his sour expression.

"As I understand it, you're the Manager of Decryption of Images and Records."

He nodded.

"Can you please tell me who reports directly to you?"

"The Supervisor of Processing and my administrative assistant." His cadence was curt, even icy.

Sanders picked up the Delta Organization Chart.
"That would be, respectively, Jane Bonham and
Cathy Cooper."

"That's correct."

Sanders set the chart back down on his desk.
"What about the Supervisor of Quality Control?" He
wanted to make certain to corroborate the information provided by the gatekeeper.

Delman shook his head. "Right now, we don't
have one, and if we did, he or she would report to the
Account Manager."

Sander leaned back in his chair. "After visiting
with your counterparts in the other accounts, I have
a fairly good grasp how your area works. However, I
just wanted to clarify a few things. As I understand,
your area receives the encrypted data through one
system from the delivery servers, correct?"

Delman shifted in his chair. "Yes, it's our responsibility to decrypt the data and send it on to Batching
of Records and Files."

Sanders narrowed his eyes. "When you decrypt
the data, is it entered into just the one system to send
to Batching of Records and Files?"

He grimaced. "No, that would be too simple. We
load it into two systems. One goes to Batching and
the other goes offsite."

Sanders stifled a gasp. That was the first time he
had heard the second system went offsite. "Did you

say the second system sends the data offsite?"

Delman nodded. "Yes, I learned that from the Account Manager."

Sanders jotted on his legal pad. "He told you the system carried the data outside of Global Data Systems?"

Delman glanced around as one might do in a crowd of people to see who was nearby before he spoke. "On my fifth work anniversary, the Account Manager took me to dinner at Chamberlain's Steakhouse. We split a bottle of wine for dinner. He then suggested we have another drink at the bar. Well, one drink turned into about three. That's when he told me about the other system going offsite."

Sanders raised an eyebrow. "Did he state a purpose for sending it out of Global Data Systems?"

Delman sighed. "No, I think he realized he had inadvertently shared some confidential information and clammed up."

"I don't suppose he revealed the destination of where the data was sent?"

"As I recall, he said it was sent to the Dallas site."

Sanders wrinkled his forehead. "To the Dallas site?"

He nodded.

"Any idea where?"

Delman shrugged. "Beats me."

"Did he possibly give any reason for even having a second system?"

He shook his head. "Nope."

"Could it be for safekeeping?"

"He never said anything about safekeeping."

Sanders scratched on his legal pad. "Delman, I think that's all the questions I have for you. Thank you for your time."

After Delman left his office, Sanders leaned back in his chair to ponder.

What possible purpose would it serve to send all that decrypted data to an offsite location? That's a very risky thing to do with private health information!

He tugged on his left ear lobe. *I need to find out if that practice is true and if so, where the data ends up in Dallas.*

Sanders' cell phone buzzed on his desk. He glanced down at the screen and grabbed it right away. "Hello, Agent Hale."

"Mr. Pierce, do you have a few minutes to talk."

"Yes."

"Forensics recovered the bullet from the tree over at UT Dallas."

Sanders thought he could detect the tenseness in her voice. "That's good, isn't it?"

She sighed. "It's good they recovered it. The bad news is that it was fired from an altered high power sniper rifle. The person who took a shot at you is no crackpot. I'm convinced more than ever that the shooting is related to your work at Global Data Systems. That's, of course, unless there is some other reason you've not shared with me that a professional killer is after you."

A pit hardened in his stomach. "I assure you, Agent Hale, I'm not aware of anyone who would want to kill me."

"Are you anywhere near finishing your investigation at Global Data Systems?"

He leaned forward in his chair. "Without violating attorney client privilege, I can inform you that I'm tracking down some credible leads which might result in the conclusion of my assignment."

Agent Hale groaned. "The closer you get to finding a culprit for the leaked data, the more danger you're likely in."

Sanders scribbled on his legal pad. "I understand, Agent Hale."

"Is there anything you can possibly share with me without violating your client's privilege?"

"I'm sorry but not at this time, not unless my client allows me to waive the privilege."

"Who in the corporation would have to approve the waiver?"

"The General Counsel may possibly be empowered to waive it, but I suspect she would want approval from the president. You realize, though, I would be required to inform my client I'm disclosing this confidential information to the FBI."

"We don't want our involvement revealed at this time," Agent Hale snapped. "It would tip off the culprits and make our job that much harder."

"I understand. However, I promise you, should I discover any illegal activity which is outside the scope of any privilege, I'll immediately contact you."

"Thank you, Mr. Pierce."

Sanders sent an email to the Gamma gatekeeper, requesting an interview with the Quality Control Supervisor. He was cognizant she reported directly to the Account Manager. She could be a valuable source of information to confirm the reasoning for the offsite Dallas facility.

When his cell phone chimed, Sanders picked it up. A text from Claire said:

> I hope you are free for dinner tonight at 7:00 p.m. Dress spiffy!

* * *

Sanders was not sure what Claire meant by 'spiffy'. He put on a pair of dark slacks and a light blue shirt and topped it off with an Armani sport coat that he had splurged for when he was practicing law full time.

At 6:55 p.m., his doorbell rang. He hurried down from the third floor and opened the door. Claire stood smiling on his porch under the porch light. She wore a black cocktail dress.

Sanders eyes widened. "I don't think I have ever seen you out of uniform. You look quite lovely."

She bowed her head a bit. "Thank you, I was hoping it was warm enough to wear this dress. Also, you look very un-lawyer like."

He snickered. "I'll take that as a compliment. By the way, where are we going for dinner?"

Claire winked at him. "It's a surprise. Do you mind driving?"

As soon as they exited the gate of their community, Claire said, "Go south on the North Dallas Toll Road."

Sanders drove the short distance south on Mimosa and took a right on Campbell Road. Several blocks west, he followed a circuitous route he had stumbled upon a few months earlier. He took a left on Amberwood Road, left on Brentfield, and right on Keller Springs Road, which intersected the North Dallas Toll Road.

Glancing in his rearview mirror several times, Sanders noticed a black car following him that made every single turn as well. "I think the guy behind me has discovered my secret short cut to the North Dallas Toll Road. Either that or we're being followed."

Claire said, "Let's see if the guy follows us where I'm taking you."

He glanced over at her. "Are you ready yet to tell me where we're going?"

"Nope."

When they had reached just south of the Mockingbird Lane exit, Claire said, "Take the Oak Lawn exit and get in the left lane."

"I'm surprised. I thought we were heading downtown."

Sanders peeked at his rearview mirror. The car

took the Oak Lawn Avenue exit as well. At the stop light, Claire said turn left.

"Are we going to a restaurant in Oak Lawn?"

She tapped his knee. "Patience."

They continued several more blocks on Oak Lawn Avenue. Claire instructed him to slow down and take a right on Gillespie Street. At that moment it occurred to Sanders where they were dining tonight.

"Oh my God, we're going to The Mansion, aren't we?"

Claire laughed. "Very perceptive, counselor."

Sanders peeked at his side mirror. The car also turned onto Gillespie Street. "That black car is still trailing us."

She glanced over her shoulder. "Do you suppose it's the FBI?"

Sanders groaned. "I prefer them over the alternative."

He eased the Spider into the driveway in front of The Mansion and right away a valet greeted him. As Sanders exited the car, he spotted the black car inching past on Gillespie until it disappeared.

He and Claire strolled up to the entrance of the restaurant.

"I guess the FBI, or whoever was tailing us, isn't having dinner at The Mansion," Claire said. "Also, dinner tonight is curtesy of Dr. Carswell."

Sanders wrinkled his forehead. "Whose Dr. Carswell and why is he paying for our dinner?"

"He's one of my clients." She smiled. "After our

last appointment, he said he wanted to gift a dinner at The Mansion for me and my boyfriend."

His eyes widened. "So, am I your boyfriend?"

Claire giggled. "No, but you're as close to a boyfriend that I have."

Sanders gave her a fake frown. "Now my feelings are hurt."

She poked him in the arm. "You'll get over it after you've had a wonderful dinner."

* * *

After dinner, Claire suggested a cocktail in the bar before heading home. The bar was about half full. They chose to sit at a two-top near the wall with a view of the rest of the bar. Both ordered a glass of Ramey Chardonnay.

An athletic statuesque woman dressed in black slacks and a red blouse approached their table. She had earlier been sitting at the end of the bar by herself. Her dark black hair just hit her shoulders.

Her eyes were laser focused on Sanders. "Sanders Pierce?"

Sanders raised an eyebrow. "Yes, that's me."

"I thought so. Have a good evening." She turned and hurried out of the bar.

Sander said, "That's very strange."

"Do you know her?"

He shrugged. "I don't think I've ever laid eyes on her."

Claire snickered. "Well, she certainly knows you. And I recall that time you said I was mysterious. You're *definitely* the mysterious one."

* * *

Sanders set his iPad on the nightstand and closed his eyes.

Who was that woman? Was she in the car that was following us?

Chapter 17

Thursday morning, Sanders pulled up his Global Data Systems email. The first email was from the Gamma gatekeeper. She had managed to arrange an interview with Debra Brannon, the Quality Control Supervisor of Gamma for 3:00 p.m.

The second email caught his attention. It was from Emma Peel. He opened it.

> I must be evasive to protect myself.
> Emma

Sanders rubbed his chin.

Does that statement mean Emma Peel fears retribution if she is discovered helping with the investigation?

He wanted to investigate further the lead Delman Jenkins had provided regarding an offsite location where the other system transferred private health information. Sanders fired off an email to the Delta gatekeeper, requesting an interview with Preston Zimmerman, Account Manager. He suspected he would be told Preston Zimmerman was not available. However, he felt he had to give it a try.

Sanders then emailed Lisa Hall, administrative

assistant to Dan Wooten and requested a second interview.

Debra Brannon arrived five minutes early for the 3:00 p.m. interview. She was a petite woman wearing a white blouse and charcoal gray coat with matching skirt. Her eyes darted around the room as she made her way over to a client chair.

Sanders sensed her discomfort. "Thank you for meeting with me."

She forced a slight smile.

"So, you're the Supervisor of Quality Control for the Gamma Account."

Debra nodded. "That's correct."

Sanders looked down at his legal pad. "As I understand, you and Mary Teague in the Beta Account are currently the only two Quality Control Supervisors since the one for the Delta Account is vacant."

She stared at Sanders. "Yes. The Delta Account currently has a vacancy at that position."

"I'm hoping you can help me understand something. Why does Mary report to the Manager of Decryption and you report all the way up to the Account Manager? In other words, why would one account treat the position differently than the other?"

Debra sighed. "I have been in this position over ten years and have more experience than my counterpart in Beta."

He wrinkled his forehead. "But don't you still do the same type of work? It seems like you would both report to the same level of manager?"

She shrugged. "That's the only explanation I can give you."

"Let me switch gears here." Sanders leaned back in his chair. "As the Quality Control Supervisor, I would think you're familiar with all aspects of how the Gamma Account operates. Is that a correct assumption?"

Debra folded her arms across her chest. "Yes, I'm familiar with all aspects of Gamma."

"When I interviewed George Atkins, the Manager of Decryption for Gamma, he indicated his department receives the encrypted data in one system. Is that your understanding as well?"

"Of course."

"George said that after the data is decrypted, it's then entered into two systems. One system goes to the Batching Department and the other goes somewhere else. Can you shed some light on the destination of the second system?"

Debra leaned forwarded and grabbed his legal pad and flipped through it to a blank page. She fished a pen out of her bag and wrote:

> All I can say is caution, things are not always as they seem.

She turned the legal pad around and slid it over to Sanders. He read it and jotted:

> I don't understand.

She again grabbed the legal pad and scribbled:

Please consider it. I believe someone is
listening.

Sanders surmised Debra feared their conversation was being overheard. He felt a desperate urge
to ask her about the Dallas offsite but decided not to
broach the subject yet. Perhaps he could arrange a
meeting with her offsite. Sanders jotted on the legal
pad.

"Can you meet me offsite to continue our
discussion?"

Debra shook her head.

He decided to end the interview. "Okay, Debra.
On second thought. I don't need to ask you anything
about the second system. That is all the questions I
have at this time."

She mouthed, "Thank you."

After she exited the office, Sanders leaned back in
his chair to think about what just happened.

*What was that all about? Did somebody bug my
office?* His eyes shifted from side to side. *If so, how
did she know?*

He stood up from his desk and scanned the entire
office. It was in the same condition as when he first
moved in. The walls were bare of any artwork. The
only furniture in the office was a small credenza,

the desk, a single desk chair, and two client chairs. He could not fathom where someone could plant a listening device.

Sanders turned over his desk chair to inspect under the seat. Nothing there except the levers that controlled the height and lumbar support.

Next, he felt under the edges of his desk and then even got down on his hands and knees to inspect under it. Sanders laid both client chairs on their sides so he could see the underside. He checked all the nooks and crannies of the credenza and at last opened all his desk drawers.

If the office is bugged, I sure as hell can't locate it. Maybe Debra was being overly suspicious.

He plopped back down in his desk chair when he had a sudden epiphany. Sanders scrolled though his emails. He pulled up the first email he had received from Emma Peel.

Caution! Things are not always as they seem!

My God, Debra Brannon is Emma Peel! She knows something and she's afraid because of it!

Sanders sent an email to Jackie, requesting a brief meeting. He wanted to ask her for either a new office or to have the existing office checked for a listening device but did not want to address it in the email, in case someone was monitoring it.

It was almost 5:00 p.m. and Sanders doubted if Jackie would respond before morning. He put all his papers into his briefcase, preparing to leave for the day. As soon as Sanders reached for doorknob on his door, the phone on the desk rang. It rang so seldom that it always startled him. He raced back over to his desk and picked up the receiver. "Hello."

"Hi, Sanders. What's up?"

"Hi, Jackie. Can we meet in person? I think it might be preferable than discussing this issue over the phone.

He detected a sigh at the other end of the line. "Can this wait until tomorrow morning?"

"Of course."

"I've got an opening at 10:00 a.m., so I can meet you at your office then."

"Great. I'll see you in the morning."

Chapter 18

Sanders was glad it was Friday. He glanced at his watch. It was 10:05 a.m. He surmised Jackie had something come up, which caused her to be late for their meeting.

At 10:35 a.m. three knocks came on his office door. As was her custom, Jackie opened the door and turned to close it behind her.

Sanders said, "Do you mind if we step outside just a second?" He opened the door and edged into the hallway.

She wrinkled her forehead but followed him. "Sanders, why are we meeting outside your office?"

He sighed. "I think it's possible someone has it bugged."

"You mean like a listening device?"

Sanders nodded. "Precisely. I feel like I'm getting closer to finding a lead on the leaks. If someone is listening to my interviews, I don't want them to know what I know."

Jackie scowled. "Okay, I'll ask Corporate Security to look into it."

"Jackie, I might be onto something major here and I don't know who's involved. Is it possible to get some expert outside of Global Data Systems?"

"Do you know anyone?"

He shook his head. "No, but I'll find someone."

"Very well. Let Beverly know his name and she can get him access to the Global Data System campus and can authorize payment for his services. Now, can you brief me on your lead?"

"I can, but I would prefer to wait to see if it pans out. I may be completely off base."

Jackie pursed her lips. "In that case, I need to get back upstairs. I've a lot on my plate to deal with."

Sanders spent the better part of the day searching for someone who could hunt through his office for any possible listening device. He contacted a national company with a Dallas branch that specialized in accredited bug sweeps and professional eavesdropping detection services.

He was able to get an appointment for Monday morning at 9:00 a.m. but with an assessed emergency fee of $10,000 for a space the size of his office. He hoped Jackie did not hit the roof when she learned the amount.

He spent the remainder of the afternoon reading over his notes for the entire time he had been on this assignment. Sanders wanted to make sure he had not missed something obvious. He pulled up his email for one final look before shutting down for the weekend.

Two unopened emails waited in his inbox. The first one was from Beverly, indicating Jackie had mentioned the need to have a visitor approved.

The second one was from Emma Peel.

Tonight, at The Lodge. You know the Dallas location.

Sanders rubbed his head. *That's obtuse, even for Emma Peel. What's The Lodge?*

He did a quick search on the internet and discovered that The Lodge was an upscale "gentleman's" club. He presumed that was a euphemistic way of saying that The Lodge is a fancy strip club.

Why did Emma mention The Lodge?

He snapped his fingers and grinned.

The second sentence must be a reference to the Dallas offsite location where the private health information is sent. His eyes lit up. *But a strip club? Surely, that can't be the case.*

* * *

Sanders arrived back at his gated community at 5:30 p.m. As he rounded the curb onto Grove Park Lane, he spotted Claire at her mailbox. Claire must have noticed his Spider because she waited for him to drive up.

When Sanders pulled up alongside her, he rolled down his window. "I see by your yoga pants and runners you're glad the week is almost over. Happy Friday."

She sighed. "I don't know about you, but I'm so ready for the weekend."

"Any big plans?"

Claire shook her head. "No, what about you?"

He smiled. "Would you like to go to dinner tonight?"

"Sure," she giggled, "as long as we're going to The Mansion."

Sanders chuckled. "No, I had something different in mind. Actually, I want to go to a place that may be related to the temporary assignment I'm on."

She cocked her head and gave him a puzzled frown. "What does that mean?"

He was careful not to reveal any client confidential information. "Ever heard of The Lodge in northwest Dallas?"

Claire squinted as if that would jar a memory. "No, I can't say that I have."

"According to its website and I quote, 'The Lodge has built a famous reputation for its rustic elegance, superb cuisine, and unparalleled southern hospitality, featuring the most beautiful entertainers from around the world.' In other words, it's an upscale strip joint."

She rolled her eyes. "You must have spent quite some time on the website to have memorized that description."

He feigned embarrassment. "I had to perform some due diligence research."

"Let's see if I got this straight. I take you to The Mansion and you want to take me to a strip club instead, is that correct?"

His jaw muscles tensed. "I guess that was a lousy

idea. I apologize for asking."

Claire walked over and gave his arm a light smack. "I'm just playing with you. Sure, I'll go to dinner with you at The Lodge. I love new and unusual experiences."

He exhaled in relief. "I thought I had offended you."

She smiled. "Not at all. But I do have one question. How can an upscale strip club have anything to do with your assignment at Global Data Systems?"

Sanders grimaced. "Without violating the attorney client privilege, all I can say is I got a tip."

Claire glanced down at her watch. "What time did you want to leave?"

"Does 6:45 p.m. work for you?"

She gave him a thumbs up. "I'll change into something more appropriate."

* * *

Sanders eased his Spider into the driveway outside of The Lodge. All the parking spaces had orange cones, so he pulled up to the entrance and a valet met him.

At least I can recognize him by his standard uniform.

As Sanders exited the car, the valet said, "Would you like to have your car washed?"

Sanders handed him the keys. "How much does that cost?"

"Thirty dollars, plus tip."

"Sure. Go for it."

Sanders had not been certain how to dress for the evening, so he wore a pair of charcoal gray slacks, blue dress shirt, and a dark blue sport coat. Claire wore something similar. Sanders thought she looked lovely but suspected that the two of them would be mistaken for undercover cops by the predominantly all-male clientele.

The detailed website description of a luxurious rustic lodge was spot on. In the front room, he looked up at a solid cedar wood cathedral ceiling complemented with mounted heads of various animals. It resembled an upscale hunting lodge except for the scantily clad women serving drinks and the female dancers on different stages in various degrees of undress.

Sanders asked the hostess for a seat in a quiet area.

She said, "The V.I.P. area upstairs is the quietest location, but it'll cost you fifty dollars."

Sanders sighed. "That's fine. We'll sit there."

As they followed the hostess through the front area of The Lodge, Sanders felt as if every eye in the place was laser focused upon them.

"If one of these guys touches me," Claire whispered, "he's going to lose a hand."

Sanders snickered. "I don't doubt you one bit."

The hostess led them upstairs to a square room that opened to the room below. She pointed at a table in the corner. "That's probably our quietest table."

Sanders and Claire sat next to one another with their backs to the wall, giving both of them a view of the surroundings.

A server approached their table with menus and took their drink order.

"Well," Sanders said, "what do you think so far of The Lodge?"

She flipped her hair over her shoulder. "My first impression is that the décor is a bit trashy, albeit expensive."

"That's an interesting perspective. I hope the food is palatable. Let's look at the menus."

Sanders opted for the cedar plank salmon and Claire selected a trout dish.

"Although I don't eat meat," she said, "after seeing all those stuff animal heads in the front room, I feel almost compelled to order steak."

He laughed. "I was thinking the same thing."

Both sampled their entrees, then dug in with healthy appetites.

"I have to admit," Claire said, "I didn't think the food would be any good, but that trout was very tasty."

Sanders nodded. "Mine, too." He paused. "To change the subject, I've no idea how this place could be in any way linked to my investigation at Global Data Systems."

Before Claire could respond, a young lady wearing a black micro mini skirt approached their table. She smiled. "I'm Shay. Do you mind if I sit down?"

Claire said, "Are you one of the entertainers?"

She glanced around. "Yes, I'm one of the dancers. Will you please buy me a drink when the server returns?"

Sanders and Claire looked at each other. Claire winked at Sanders and said, "This gentleman would love to buy you a drink."

Shay patted Sanders on the hand. "Thank you. That's the only way I can sit here unless I'm performing a table dance for one of you."

Sanders' eyes widened. "I see."

The server returned and took Shay's drink order.

"Shay's an interesting name," Claire said. "Is it a family name?"

Shay shook her head. "No, that's just my stage name. My real name is Cecelia."

The server returned with a vodka and soda with a slice of lemon and placed it on a napkin in front of Shay. She took a gulp of the drink and then said, "Are you Sanders Pierce?"

His mouth dropped open. "Yes. How did you know?"

Shay looked over her shoulder and for a few seconds scanned the immediate area around them. "My older sister is Emma Peel."

Claire wrinkled her forehead. "Emma Peel?"

Sanders said, "An informant of sorts in my investigation." He turned to stare at Shay. "How did you know what I look like?"

She took a sip of her cocktail. "You're all over the internet. It threw my sister off for a while because she didn't know you had transitioned from practicing law into art. When she found your picture on your artist website, she was certain it was you."

Sanders glanced over at Claire. "My picture is on the 'Bio' page of my website."

"I've seen your website." Claire smiled. "By the way, you were much younger looking then."

He groaned. "I know. I'll get around soon to updating it with a more current picture."

"My sister wanted me to tell you," Shay said, "that the warehouse directly across the street is the Dallas offsite. I don't know what that means but she said you would understand."

Sanders raised an eyebrow. "I think I do understand." He fished his wallet out of his pocket and pulled out five twenty-dollar bills and handed them to Shay. "I appreciate the information."

She smiled. "Thank you, but that's not really necessary."

Claire said, "Shay, he insists."

Shay took the money and stood up. "I need to get back to work." She walked away.

Sanders grimaced. "It's been an expensive night."

Patting his arm. Claire cackled. "You haven't even gotten the bill for dinner yet."

"Let's get the check and get out of here while I still have the shirt on my back."

She jerked her head to one side. "What's 'the

Dallas offsite'?"

He shrugged. "I'm not one hundred percent certain but I intend to find out."

Chapter 19

Saturday morning, Sanders stopped his car in front of The Lodge. Its parking lot next to the curb was deserted this time of day.

He eased the Spider into the parking lot of the warehouse directly across the street. Only a couple of cars were parked near the front entrance.

Sanders decided to walk around the perimeter of the warehouse to get an idea of its size. He guessed it to be about five thousand square feet.

Right behind the first warehouse were two other warehouses of the same size. Each warehouse had a separate address. The one nearest the street was Suite 100, 10531 Spangler Road, followed by Suite 200, 10531 Spangler Road and Suite 300, 10531 Spangler Road.

Sanders wondered if the Dallas offsite location was in all three or just one of the warehouses.

The dancer, Shay, had said only the warehouse across the street. He retraced his steps and approached the door in the front of the building. He paused at the entrance to scan the building for security cameras. One was positioned over the front door at the top of the one-story building. A card reader was by the door but no doorbell.

Sanders knocked several times. He was about to give up when the door slid ajar. A uniformed security guard peered through the crack in the door. "Can I help you?"

Sanders feigned a smile. "Good morning. I was told this was the address where my client has some files stored."

The security guard frowned. "I don't know anything about files. I just guard the premises."

"Can you tell me what it looks like inside?"

The security guard narrowed his eyes. "It looks like just like any other warehouse I've ever seen. I only patrol outside the office area."

Sanders attempted to look over the security guard's shoulder but could not see anything. "Any idea what they do here?"

He shook his head. "No clue. As I said, I just guard the premises."

Sanders sensed the security guard was growing impatient with his questions. "One last question, do you happen to know if the same business operates in all three of the warehouses or just this one?"

"Look, mister, as I said, I just guard this building. I don't know anything about the other warehouses."

The security guard slammed the door.

Sanders approached the front door of the next building in Suite 200. No security cameras were visible on the exterior of the building. He knocked on the door and waited several minutes before walking over to Suite 300.

The same as Suite 200, no security cameras anywhere in sight. Sanders again knocked but with the same result.

I guess I'll have to wait until next week.

He headed back to his car, glancing over his shoulder as he walked. *Is something unlawful going on here? I don't have enough credible information to involve the FBI.*

* * *

Late Saturday afternoon, Sanders pulled into the parking lot in front of Interurban Contemporary, his art gallery that he had more or less abandoned while on this assignment. Taylor's car sat parked next to the front entrance.

He opened the door and walked inside. All the gallery lights were on and electronic ambient music booming from the various speakers throughout.

He shouted, "Taylor, are you here?"

A few seconds later she came bounding around the corner from the back of the gallery. "Sorry, I was in back rearranging some of the stored art."

Sanders smiled. "No problem. How are you doing?"

She flipped her hair back out of her eyes. "I'm doing fine. How's the assignment going?"

"Very interesting, to the say the least."

"Are you almost finished with it?"

He sighed. "I'm not sure. Things might break open in the next few days or on the other hand, it may go on awhile."

Taylor's eyes lit up. "I've some good news! I was

accepted as an intern at the De Menil Collection in Houston!"

"That's fantastic Taylor. So, when do you start?"

She wrinkled her nose. "They want me to start in three weeks. I'm sorry, Sanders. I know you might not be finished with your assignment by then."

Sanders patted her shoulder. "Not a problem at all. I'm just so excited for you. There's only one downside to your moving to Houston."

"What's that?"

He cracked half a grin. "Humidity. Brace yourself when summer rolls around. It can be unbearable down there."

She smiled. "Well, I'll have several months to prepare for it, since I'm not moving until November."

Sanders gestured toward the bar. "Let's get a glass of wine to celebrate."

He poured them two glasses of Sonoma Cutrer Chardonnay and they settled down on two of the stools at the bar.

"I'm glad you came in," Taylor said. "Do you remember that woman who came in and asked about you several days ago?"

He nodded. "Of course. Did she come back?"

"Not inside. But I could have sworn she was sitting in her car in the parking lot across the street when I left the gallery yesterday."

Sanders raised an eyebrow. "Really? Why do you think it was her?"

Taylor rubbed her chin. "First, she was parked at

the end of the lot away from the building. I thought that was an odd place to park. Also, I got just a glimpse of her face when I drove by. Although she was wearing sunglasses, I recognized that sneer she gave me the other day."

"Do you recall what kind of car she was driving?"

She nodded. "Yes, I recognized the BMW logo on the front. It was a black BMW sedan."

"Great. Were you able to get the license number?"

Taylor shook her head.

Chapter 20

Monday morning, Sanders arrived at his office at 8:30 a.m. He had thirty minutes before the contractor he hired to sweep his office for any listening devices was due to arrive. Sanders accessed his email and found a message from Lisa Hall.

She indicated she was available Monday afternoon at 2:00 p.m. for a meeting. He sent a response confirming the time.

Another email from Emma Peel popped up.

> I wanted to confirm that Shay made the right connection.
> Emma

He sent a brief response, confirming that the connection was made.

At 9:05 a.m., Jackie's administrative assistant, Beverly, and another woman appeared at his doorway.

"Sanders," Beverly said, "this is Jan Stark of Meticulous Detection Services."

Jan was a petite thin blond woman dressed in a gray pantsuit and white blouse, carrying a black leather satchel.

Sheesh, she could get a job here just based on her wardrobe.

Sanders guessed her to be in her early thirties. Jan handed Sanders a card.

Beverly said, "I'll leave you two alone," and exited the office.

"Thank you for coming on such short notice. So, where do we start?"

She set her satchel on the floor. "First, I'm going to do a visual inspection of the premises. Second, I will conduct an inspection with one or more detection tools. If there's a listening device, I'll find it."

Sanders gestured toward his desk chair. "Will I be in the way if I sit down?"

"Why don't you sit in one of your client chairs. I want to start with your computer and then I'll move to the desk, credenza, etc."

He slid into the client chair nearest the door.

Jan sat down in the desk chair. "I see you have your email open. I'm not going to read any of your mail, I just need to check the filters to see if anything is suspicious there."

After several seconds, she said, "I assume your email address is S.Pierce@GDS.com."

Sanders nodded. "Yes, that's me."

She looked up from the screen. "Would you come take a look at this?"

He walked around the desk and peered over her shoulder.

"Do you see those two dots?"

Sanders squinted. "Yes, I see them."

"I assume you didn't add that address."

"I'm not sure what you mean. But no, I didn't add anything."

"It's possible this account has been added so someone else can monitor your email. Should I delete it?"

"Sure."

Jan deleted it and checked several other settings. "I think it's clean now."

Sanders walked back around the desk and plopped into the client chair.

Next, Jan conducted a visual search of the desk, credenza, desk chair, similar to what Sanders had done last week. She pointed to the surge protector under his desk. "Has this surge protector always been here?"

He wrinkled his forehead. "As far as I know. I never really noticed it before."

"Okay, I'll get back to that in a minute. I want to scan the room with one of my detection tools."

She opened her satchel and connected what resembled a small vacuum cleaner head on an extension rod. Jan started in the corner of the room and checked every square inch of the drop-down ceiling tile. Satisfied with her search, she then ran the device along the floor with the same amount of thoroughness.

When she was done, she disassembled the tool

and placed it back in her satchel, and then pulled out a set of small screwdrivers. "I'm going to take a look inside the surge protector."

She unplugged the protector from the wall, turned it upside down, and removed four miniscule screws on the bottom.

Once all the screws were out, she popped the bottom cover off and stared inside a moment. "Bingo!"

Sanders hurried around to her side of the desk. She pointed with the head of the screwdriver. "See that little bugger? That's a listening device."

He bent over to get a closer look. "Can you remove it?"

She fished a pair of tweezers out of her coat and pried it off and then handed it to Sanders.

He held it up to the light and turned it over. "Is it still working."

Jan shook her head. "No, it's disabled."

Sanders slipped the device into his briefcase for safekeeping.

Jan turned the desk phone upside down and loosened the screws and then removed the bottom panel. She poked around inside with a screwdriver and clamped the bottom back in place. "It's clean."

As soon as Jan had completed her work, Sanders sent an email to Jackie, requesting a meeting that afternoon if possible.

* * *

Promptly at 2:00 p.m., Lisa arrived at Sanders' office for their meeting. He stood when she entered his office. "Thank you for meeting with me again."

She gave a slight bow of her head. "Of course."

Sanders waited for her to get settled in a chair before speaking. "How are things going with you?"

"Business as usual."

He leaned forward. "Are the three account managers still in their offsite meeting?"

She shook her head. "No, Dan's back in the office this morning."

"Does he know you are meeting with me?"

"No, he's clueless where I am."

Sanders eyes narrowed. "Was he aware that you previously met with me?"

Lisa sighed. "I didn't tell him anything, but he sure was angry about something this morning."

He glanced at his legal pad. "Do you know anything about a 10531 Spangler Road?"

She wrinkled her forehead. "Yes, I filled out some paperwork for Dan to rent some space there."

"Do you know what he uses the space for?"

Lisa shrugged. "He said he needed some extra storage for antique furniture he collects."

Sanders jotted on his legal pad. "Have you ever been to this Spangler address?"

She shook her head. "No."

"As I understand, there are three separate warehouses at that location. Do you happen to know which warehouse he rented?"

She tilted her head and squinted at him. "No, but he keeps a copy of the lease in his personal files."

"Do you have access to his personal files?"

Lisa snickered. "Technically, no, but I have a key to his office, and I know he keeps the key to his filing cabinet in the bottom lefthand desk drawer."

His eyes lit up. "I don't want to get you in trouble, but would you be willing to check the exact location of where the space on Spangler is leased?"

"That won't be a problem. I can do it while he's out on one of his extended lunches."

Sanders smiled. "That would be very helpful."

She ran a hand through her blond hair. "Do you think there's a connection between that warehouse space and the leaked information?"

"I don't know, but I certainly intend to find out. And having said that, I hope you will keep this conversation confidential."

Lisa nodded. "I'll keep it confidential. I never would tell Dan."

He sighed. "There's something else you need to know. A listening device was found in my office this morning. It's possible Dan may be aware of the conversation we had in our last meeting."

Her mouth dropped open. "Are you serious?"

"I'm afraid so."

"Maybe that explains his foul mood this morning."

Sanders rested both elbows on his desk. "Lisa, if Dan's involved in some way with the leaks, you could be in harm's way."

She sighed. "I can handle Dan."

"I'm sure you can. But be very careful."

Lisa nodded but did not respond.

"I think that's all the questions I had for you. Thank you again."

Lisa stood up. "Is it safe for me to email the address of the space Dan rented?"

Sanders paused to consider the question. "Yes, but out of an abundance of caution, do not specifically reference the Spangler address. I just need to know the suite number. So, if it's Suite 300, just make up some reason in a sentence to use the number three hundred. That way, we will be certain no one else knows what we're discussing."

"Will do."

* * *

Jackie agreed to meet with Sanders that afternoon at 4:30 p.m. She walked into his office at 4:45 p.m. "Sorry to be late." She slid into the nearest client chair.

"No, problem."

"Beverly told me the contractor you engaged to sweep your office for listening devices came by this morning.

He nodded. "Yes. She conducted a thorough search."

"I assume she didn't find anything."

Sanders frowned. "To the contrary." He stood

and fished the listening device out of his briefcase and handed it to Jackie. "Not only did she find this beauty, but she found an additional address in the filters of my email."

She examined the device. "Where did she find it?"

He pointed down below his desk. "It was in the surge protector."

Jackie's face dropped. "Oh my God. I can't believe someone would bug your office. I agreed to allow you have someone check for devices just to put your mind at ease. No way did I fathom any would actually be found."

Sanders sighed. "I think these leaks may be a bigger problem than you anticipated. No telling who's involved and how far up the corporate ladder it may go."

She narrowed her eyes. "Do you have any possible suspects?"

"Yes," he said as he leaned forward, "but I'm not one hundred percent certain."

"I don't care if you aren't one hundred percent certain. Who do think may be involved?"

Sanders rubbed his bald head. "I think that Dan Wooten, the Beta Account Manager, may be involved and possibly the account managers of Delta and Gamma."

Jackie groaned. "Oh no! That's all the accounts that handle client sensitive health information.

He nodded. "Yep."

Have you met with any of the account managers?"

Sanders shook his head. "No, I've tried, but so far they've been unavailable."

She wrinkled her forehead. "What have you found that makes these guys suspects?"

He picked up the Beta Account's Health Claims Processing Workflow Chart and pointed to the system feeding encrypted data to the Decryption of Images and Records Department. "Remember in an earlier meeting when I told you there's only one system going into Decryption but two systems going out? I have been given all kinds of vague answers to the purpose of the second system."

Jackie nodded. "Yes."

Sanders took a deep breath. "In one of my interviews, I learned that the second system sends the data offsite to a location in Dallas."

Her right eyebrow shot up. "Offsite to a Dallas location?"

"That's correct. Do you remember the mysterious emails I received from Emma Peel?"

"Yes, I remember."

His eyes lit up. "Well, she didn't come right out and tell me who she is, but she did give me enough clues to deduce her identity. Anyway, Emma Peel arranged for a third party to give me the potential location of the Dallas offsite."

Jackie rubbed her forehead. "What do you mean 'a third party'?"

He grimaced. "A stripper, who happens to be Emma's sister."

She rolled her eyes. "I don't know, Sanders. This is starting to sound a little hokey. Where did you meet this stripper?"

Sanders bowed his head a bit and tried not to blush. "At The Lodge. It's a gentleman's club in northwest Dallas."

Jackie pursed her lips. "Let's assume, for the sake of argument, this lead is real. What's your next move?"

"The offsite location is directly across the street from The Lodge. Unfortunately, three warehouse suites are at that address. If I can pinpoint the correct one, I want to pay it a visit during business hours."

She heaved a huge sigh. "I don't want you getting into any danger."

His eyes widened. "Regrettably, I think it's too late to worry about that. Someone has already taken a shot at me."

Jackie was laser focused on him. "Are you kidding?"

Sanders shook his head. "No, it happened over on the UT Dallas campus early one morning. I jog over there around the soccer fields. Afterwards, I usually walk back to my house along this isolated pathway. Midway down the path, I noticed my shoe had come untied. When I kneeled to tie it, I heard a crack over my head and a bullet slam into the trunk of a nearby tree."

"You don't think that incident is related to your assignment here, do you?"

He was careful not to mention the FBI by name. "The authorities indicated there may be a connection."

She cocked her head to the side. "How so?"

"Are you aware of the Manager of Decryption in the Beta Account who was murdered in his driveway?"

Jackie nodded. "Of course, the Plano police were on campus, questioning several employees."

He groaned. "That's the connection. The same person or persons who killed him may have taken a shot at me."

She sneered. "I don't know, Sanders. Without more evidence, that seems like a stretch."

"You may be right."

Jackie shifted in her chair. "If you're really concerned about your safety, I won't hold it against you if you want to walk away right now from this assignment."

Sanders feigned a smile. "Not a chance. I'm curious to see where this thing leads."

She stood up. "Just promise me you'll be careful."

He saluted her in a playful gesture. "Yes, ma'am."

After Jackie left his office, Sanders decided to check his email one last time before leaving. He opened an email from Lisa Hall.

> Mr. Pierce, I thought about the question you posed to me regarding janitorial services access to the claims processing area. I am 100 percent certain it is not a problem. The service is vetted by Corporate Security.

Sanders smiled.

The address in the lease that Dan Wooten signed is for 10531 Spangler, Suite 100!

Chapter 21

Tuesday morning, Sanders maneuvered the Spider through rush hour traffic all the way over to northwest Dallas. He cruised along Spangler Road until he arrived at 10531, then pulled into the parking lot right in front of the building and parked in the space nearest the front door.

The lot was empty except for his car. Instead of going straight to the front door, he walked around the building to the rear.

The parking lot behind Suite 100 had only six cars. Sanders surmised that at least that number of people should be inside the warehouse. The rear door to the building was a heavy-duty steel door identical to the one in front. A security camera near the roof pointed at the area surrounding the door. No doorbell, same as the front, and a card reader was mounted on the wall next to the door.

He knocked several times on the door and took a few steps backwards, glancing up at the security camera. No one answered the door.

I know there's got to be someone inside. Why won't anyone come to the door?

Sanders strode around the entire exterior of the building, hoping to find a window or see some form of life inside. Gritting his teeth, he returned to his Spider and headed north in the direction of Global Data Systems. His first order of business for the day was to send an email to Lisa Hall. He pondered what to say in case someone was still monitoring his email.

> Ms. Hall, I apologize but I had a few follow up questions concerning which individuals have security access to the area of the Beta Account where incoming documents are scanned. Are you available to meet with me? I won't keep you too long.
> Thank you.
> Sanders Pierce

He had no interest in that area but thought it would not arouse suspicion on anyone's part.

Lisa responded ten minutes later, indicating she was available at 12:30 p.m. Sanders wondered if she chose that time because she knew Dan Wooten would be at lunch. Lisa Hall arrived at his office promptly at 12.30 p.m. She was dressed impeccably but her eyes were bloodshot.

Sanders said, "Thank you for coming."

She did not say anything but plopped down in a client chair.

"Lisa, is everything all right?'

Lisa exhaled. "No, Dan's transferring me out of Beta. I think he knows what we discussed in our first meeting when your office was bugged."

He frowned. "I'm very sorry. If that proves to be the case, then it's almost a slam dunk he's involved in something nefarious."

A tear rolled down her cheek. "I hate that man."

"At least you don't have to work with him anymore." Sanders leaned back in his chair. "Is this a lateral transfer for you?"

She shook her head. "No, I retain my same salary, but the chance of any future advancement is nil."

He wrinkled his forehead. "So, I assume this transfer is considered a disciplinary move?"

Lisa scowled. "That's correct."

"Well, if it turns out he's involved in some illegal activity, then your stellar reputation should be restored."

She smirked. "Do you really think you'll ever get anything on him?"

Sanders nodded. "I'm certain I'm getting closer. So, when is your transfer effective?"

"Next Monday morning. I'm already cleaning out my cubicle."

He groaned. "Wow, that's quick."

"Anyway, why did you want to meet with me?"

He sighed. "Do you know anything about the card reader that unlocks the doors over at the warehouse on Spangler?"

She nodded. "Yes, I ordered them for Dan."

Sanders eyes widened. "Is there any way you can get a card for me to access the reader?"

Lisa wiped a tear from her eye. "I'm sorry, I can't

do something like that. If I got caught, I would be fired for sure."

"I understand completely, Lisa. Please forget that I asked you."

She nodded but remained silent.

He stood up. "Thank you so much for coming and all your assistance in this matter."

Lisa shot to her feet and hurried over to the door. Before opening it to exit, she turned around. "I hope you nail that bastard!"

Sanders plopped back down in his chair.

I guess I'll have to go to Plan B. Unfortunately, I don't have one.

He flipped through his notes and came across one he made about Emma Peel, which triggered a thought.

He drafted an email to Emma Peel

> Emma,
> Is there any way that you can help me get access to the location Shay mentioned?
> Thank you,
> Sanders

Sanders checked his email every ten minutes to see if Emma had responded. He considered contacting Debra Brannon but did not want to blow her cover. Finally, at 4:45 p.m., an email appeared in his inbox.

Shay would like to have a word with you. Can

you see her tonight at 9:00 p.m.?
Emma

I guess I'm going to pay The Lodge another visit tonight. He shrugged. *At least at that time of night, there should not be any traffic.*

He texted Claire to see if she would like to join him, but she declined, due to a late evening appointment. Sanders could not comprehend why anyone would schedule a session for power exchange late in the evening or why Claire would agree to it.

* * *

At 8:30 p.m., Sanders turned right on Spangler Road. The parking lot next to The Lodge was almost full. He chuckled to himself as he thought of the contrast from the morning when The Lodge looked deserted.

The prompt valet met him as he pulled the Spider up to the stand. Sanders opted to sit in the V.I.P. balcony area, the same as his only other visit.

As he followed the hostess through the front room of the club, he spotted Shay dancing on one of the stages. Men surrounded the stage, spellbound by her every move. Sanders wondered if Shay had seen him as well.

He ordered a cocktail and surveyed his surroundings. Only three other tables in the area were occupied. Sanders speculated a majority of the customers opted to be downstairs where most of the stages were located.

A young statuesque blond woman approached his table. She slid into the chair next to Sanders.

"Do you mind if I sit down?"

His eyes widened. "Actually, I'm waiting for someone."

She batted her eyes. "Is this someone a man or woman?"

"A woman."

The woman patted his arm. "Would you care for a table dance while you're waiting?"

Sanders shook his head. "No, but thank you."

She slowly rose to her feet. "You don't know what you're missing."

He watched as she slinked across the room and approached another table.

That must be the woman's modus operandi *for making money.*

Sanders checked his watch. It was now 9:15 p.m. At last, Shay came around the corner. As her eyes scanned the room, her head turned from side to side.

She plopped down in the chair next to Sanders and set a small purse on the table. "This needs to be discreet."

His eyebrows shot up. "Sure. Would you like a cocktail?"

She nodded. "You'll have to buy one if you want me to sit here for a while."

A server approached and took her order.

He said, "How have you been?"

"Fine," she snapped.

The server returned with her cocktail and placed it on small napkin in front of her.

"I'm not trying to be rude, but after tonight," Shay said, "I don't want any more part in whatever scheme you and my sister are involved in. If management thinks I'm associated with anything illegal, I'll get fired."

Sanders gasped. "Of course, Shay. I'm very sorry. I assure you, though, we're the good guys."

She rolled her eyes. "I don't care. I don't like this cloak and dagger stuff."

"Your sister is just being very careful."

Shay reached into her purse and pulled out a plastic card in a paper sheath. She placed the card on the table and slid it under her cocktail napkin. "Don't touch it until I'm out of here."

"Okay."

Shay downed the remainder of her cocktail and then jerked to her feet and flounced away.

Sanders watched until she vanished around the corner before sliding a finger under the napkin and picking up the card. He slipped it into his coat pocket.

I should have given her some money but I imagine she would have refused it.

* * *

Sanders was exhausted from the day. He put on

some sweats and lay down on his bed, intending to read awhile before getting ready for sleep. Two sharp crashes against the wall shared with Claire's spare room jolted him from his drowsy state. He swung his legs off the bed and sat still, trying to decide if he was just dreaming.

Sanders pressed an ear against the wall. Two voices argued. One was Claire's, and the other was that of a man.

Sanders slipped on his runners hurried downstairs and fished Claire's key out of his desk drawer. He paused before slipping the key into her front door.

God, I hope she doesn't hate me for doing this.

Sanders raced up the stairs and peered through a crack in the door. A chill shot down his spine when he spotted Claire tied to the apparatus she had referred to as a St. Andrew's Cross. A large man clad in a black shirt and blue jeans faced Claire, holding a whip from her collection.

Sanders detected the terror in Claire's eyes. Sometime between when Sanders first overheard the argument until he arrived, the man had gagged Claire with one of her leather gag devices.

Sanders' eyes darted around the room searching for some type of instrument he could use against the man. He spied a five-pound dumbbell on the floor and scooped it up as he sprinted toward the man's back.

Before the man could wheel around all the way, Sanders crashed the dumbbell against the right side of his head. The man crumpled and fell with a loud thud at Claire's feet. Sanders rushed over and freed Claire from her restraints.

As soon as her hands were free, she unbuckled the gag and spit it out. "Thank you, Sanders! I'm so grateful you were at home."

Sanders' heart pounded from the adrenalin. "What happened?"

Claire wiped her brow with her sleeve. "Just out of nowhere, he jumped me."

"Do you know him?"

She shook her head. "No, he's a first-time client."

Sanders managed to fumble his phone out the pocket of his sweatpants. Trembling, he dialed 911.

* * *

It was almost 1:00 a.m. before the Richardson police finished with the scene. The man turned out to be a convicted felon with an outstanding arrest warrant for failure to meet with his parole officer.

Sanders found it not surprising, though, the police were a little suspicious that Claire had a dungeon on her third floor. After some explanation, she was able to convince them she maintained a legitimate practice, and that the man had attacked her.

When the officers hauled the felon away, Claire walked with Sanders down to the first floor. She gave him a light kiss on the cheek. "I'm sure glad I gave you a key to my place."

He smiled. "Me, too. Although, I must admit,

I never thought I would have to use it under these circumstances. Also, what caused the crash against the wall?"

Claire held up her left hand, swollen around the knuckles. "My left fist. I was able to free myself temporarily from that jerk, so I hit the wall as hard as I could, hoping you would hear it."

He chuckled. "You certainly got my attention."

Chapter 22

The alarm on Sanders' phone buzzed at 6:30 a.m. He switched it off and rolled over onto his back. Sanders had only gotten about four hours of sleep because of the drama next door. He debated whether to go back to sleep or get up and go for a jog.

After a few minutes of procrastinating, Sanders rolled out of bed and pulled the curtains opened. The sun was just peaking over the horizon. He put on his sweats and runners.

It was quiet in his small community this early in the morning. Sanders launched with a brisk pace for several blocks until he reached the soccer fields on the UT Dallas campus. He pressed the exercise app on his watch and then jogged east on the gravel path that surrounds several fields. Sanders rounded the corner and headed north.

About one hundred yards ahead, he spotted a jogger heading south. As the jogger drew closer, he could see that it was a tall thin woman wearing a black hoodie and black tights. Her dark hair was pulled back into a ponytail.

When they were within a few yards of one another, she smiled and said, "Good morning."

Sanders glanced over at her. "Good morning."

He continued north on the pathway until he reached the end and then headed west. At the sound of footsteps behind him, he surmised he was about to get passed by a faster jogger.

A woman's voice behind him said, "Sanders."

He stopped, whipped his head around, and felt an intense stinging pain in the middle of his back. Everything went black.

Sanders woke up on his stomach. A sharp pressure dug into the small of his back. He tried to figure out where he was. Shifting his head to the left, he recognized a gate that led into the main UT Dallas soccer field. He realized he was lying face down on the gravel path.

A woman's voice said, "I'm going to help you stand up. But if you try anything, I'll give you another shot from my taser gun which is aimed right above where you feel my knee burrowing into your back."

He coughed and said, "Who are you?"

"That's not important," she growled. "I need to get you out of here before someone sees us."

As the woman removed her knee from his back, Sanders tried to shift his arms forward but his hands were bound by zip ties behind his back. She grabbed him under his right shoulder and lifted him until he was kneeling.

"Stand up!" the woman snarled.

Sanders struggled to his feet. He was dizzy, still feeling the effects of the taser.

She shoved him in the back. "Start walking."

He took a couple of steps forward and shifted his head to get a glimpse of the woman's face. The same person who passed by him jogging in the other direction.

Sanders and the woman walked south down the trail where Sanders had just come from. Every few steps, she shoved him in the back to hurry his pace.

He kept scanning the area to the extent possible in search of someone who might help, but the whole place was deserted except for the two of them. They reached the parking lot that borders the east side of the soccer fields about twenty yards from where they started.

The woman barked, "Go left."

Sanders stepped down off the curb onto the parking lot. Only three cars were parked in the lot. She pushed him in the direction of a black BMW sedan parked facing in the opposite direction. When they were near the car, the woman pressed a key fob and the trunk popped open. She pressed the taser gun against his back. "Get in!"

He glanced at the license plate but failed to memorize the number. "I can't get inside with my hands bound behind me."

"Turn around and face me."

Sanders did as instructed and at once recognized the woman.

My God, that's the woman who was in the bar at The Mansion.

The woman shoved him in the chest, forcing him to fall back into the trunk. She grabbed both his legs and twisted them so that he lay sideways in the trunk. She slammed down the trunk lid before he could make a move.

Sanders took a deep breath, trying to calm his nerves. He was grateful it was a cool morning so the temperature in the trunk was not too hot.

The car's engine started, and the wheels hummed over the pavement. After a minute or so, Sanders' eyes adjusted to the low level of lighting. Daylight filtered through a sliver in the seams on the side of the trunk.

Sanders tugged at the zip ties, but they were secured tight around his wrists. Almost no wiggle room to maneuver his hands.

He lay still, listening to the car engine and trying to contemplate a plan for escape. A thought struck him.

Sanders recalled a presentation sponsored by Human Resources at his old law firm. He always dreaded having to attend these mandatory presentations. An officer in the Dallas Police Department had given this particular presentation. Part of it dealt with how to escape from the trunk of a car if you were ever kidnapped. Every car made since 2002 is required to have an emergency trunk release lever inside.

Sanders managed to turn over, so he faced the trunk lid. His eyes scanned the underside of the lid until they fixed on a somewhat illuminated lever.

That's got to be the release lever. He hunched forward a bit. *But how the hell am I going to activate it with my hands bound behind my back?*

He managed to turn over on his stomach and raised his bound hands behind him as high as possible. From this angle he could not see the lever or stretch his hands high enough to have any contact with the underside of the lid.

The hum of the BMW engine, coupled with traffic noises outside, suggested the car was driving on a freeway. This lasted for about thirty minutes. He spent this time searching underneath him for anything sharp he could rub against the zip ties.

The car slowed down and came to a stop. The car door opened and slammed shut. He braced for the woman to pop open the trunk, but nothing happened.

Sanders kicked with his right foot in the direction of the emergency lever but failed to get the proper angle. He shifted his position and struck the lever with his foot.

The trunk lid popped open. The cool air felt refreshing rushing through the opening.

As fast as he could, he swung his left leg over the side of the trunk, followed by his right leg. His stomach muscles cramped as he attempted to sit up.

Sanders managed to right himself and fell knees first on the pavement. The whole effort had exhausted him. His heart pounded in his chest. Using the rear bumper as support, he stood up.

He scanned the area for any sight of the woman. She was nowhere in sight.

Sanders hurried away from the car through a parking lot. His body ached all over from lying in a cramped position in the trunk.

He made it to the alley behind a strip series of buildings. Sanders ambled to the end of the alley and spotted a street sign. He mouthed the words on the sign. "S. Madison Avenue."

Why is that name familiar?

He took a right on S. Madison Avenue as a car passed and honked at him. Sanders knew it looked odd to be walking down a sidewalk with his hands bound behind his back. He made it to the intersection and all of a sudden recognized where he was. The intersecting street was Jefferson Boulevard.

Sanders had grown up a short distance just south of here in Wynnewood North, a small neighborhood located in the Oak Cliff region of Dallas. All the stores had changed over the years, but several of the store brick facades looked the same.

It was still too early in the morning for most retail to be open. He considered trying to flag down a driver but assumed he would appear more threatening than anything.

A few doors down was the historic Texas Theatre. It was famous for being the place where the police arrested Lee Harvey Oswald on the day President John F. Kennedy was assassinated.

As soon as Sanders reached the front of the

theatre, he spotted the woman exiting a building a few yards away. He ducked into the alcove under the marquee at the theatre entrance. Sanders hoped she had not seen him.

He rushed over to the double doors on one side of the ticket booth and tried to turn the knob with his bound hands. It did not budge.

His eyes darted to the sidewalk to make sure the woman was not in sight and then tried the knob on the other door. It gave way and Sanders pushed it open with his shoulder. He stepped inside and leaned against an interior wall, panting.

Only a few lights were switched on in the lobby. The last time he recalled being in the Texas Theatre was when he was in the sixth grade. A friend from the neighborhood and he had walked to it one summer day to see *The Good, The Bad and The Ugly*, starring Client Eastwood. The memory was etched in Sanders' memory because the movie became his favorite western ever.

A man's voice shouted from across the lobby, "The theatre's not open!"

Sanders could not see anyone until the man emerged from the shadows on the other side of the lobby. "I need your help."

The man drew closer with a scowl on his face. "What kind of help?"

"I was kidnapped." Sanders twisted his body around so the man could see that his hands were bound. "Can you cut these zip ties off me?"

The man wrinkled his forehead. "How do I know you didn't just escape from the cops?"

Sanders groaned. "Sir, you've got to believe me."

"Who kidnapped you then?"

Sanders gestured with his head. "It was some woman. I was out jogging in Richardson and this woman shot me with a taser gun. She slipped these zip ties on me when I was incapacitated. Then she put me in the trunk. For whatever reason, she drove down to Oak Cliff. When she left the car, I was able to kick the emergency release and escape."

The man scratched his head. "That's a little hard to believe. I'm inclined to call the cops."

Sanders eyes widened. "You would be doing me a big favor if you would call the police."

"Listen, I'm just the custodian, I don't want to get involved—"

"Would you call the Dallas office of the FBI for me?"

The man took a step closer and studied Sanders' face. "Well, I guess if you want me to call the FBI, then you must not have escaped from the cops."

"And would you please cut these off my wrists?"

The man fished a knife out of his pocket and sliced through the plastic zip ties.

Sanders rubbed his wrists where the ties had torn into the flesh. "Thank you, sir. Is there a phone I could use?"

The man pointed over his shoulder. "There's a pay phone over there. I suppose you'll need a quarter." He pulled a quarter out of his pants' pocket and flipped it over to Sanders.

"Thanks. Listen, do you mind locking that door until the FBI gets here? It's possible the kidnapper could come in here looking for me. If that happens, you'll also be in danger."

Sanders called information and dialed the number given to him for the Dallas office of the FBI. He was patched through to Agent Hale. She sent two agents down to Oak Cliff to pick him up.

* * *

At 11:30 a.m., Sanders waited in a small meeting room at the Dallas office of the FBI. He had spent the previous thirty minutes giving all the details of his kidnapping to the two agents who picked him up in Oak Cliff.

Agent Hale strolled into the room. "Mr. Pierce, it sounds like you had a bit of excitement this morning."

He nodded. "I guess that's one way of putting it."

She sat down and pulled a pen and pad out of her bag. "I want to focus on this woman who kidnapped you. From the report, you said you recognized her from having seen her at The Mansion, is that correct?"

Sanders rubbed his wrists. "Yes, a neighbor and I went there for dinner one night. I noticed a black car following us while in route to The Mansion. It made every turn we did until we pulled into the driveway in front of the restaurant."

"Was it the same car used in the kidnapping?"

He shrugged. "It was the same color, but I can't say for certain it was the same car."

"Were you able to get the license number?"

Sanders shook his head. "I just got a brief glimpse but didn't get a chance to memorize it."

Agent Hale tapped her pen on the notepad. "Go ahead with your story."

"My friend and I decided to have a drink in the bar before heading home. This mysterious woman approached our table and asked if I was Sanders Pierce. When I responded that I was, she said 'I thought so'."

"Is that all?"

He sighed. "She wished us a good evening and exited the bar."

Agent Hale leaned forward. "She probably wanted to get a close look at your face."

"In retrospect, that's what I think, too."

She flipped through her notes. "As I recall, you said the individual who took a shot at you at UT Dallas was also driving a black car."

Sanders nodded. "Yes, a black car sped away right after the shooting. I assumed the shooter was driving it."

Agent Hale narrowed her eyes. "It's probable the shooter, the kidnapper, and the woman who inquired about you at your art gallery are the same person.

"I suspect that's correct."

"Mr. Pierce, is there anything you can tell me

about what you've found from your investigation at Global Data Systems. I know you're an attorney, but I remind you that any illegal activity or cover up of such activity by Global Data Systems is not protected by the attorney client privilege."

He paused to ponder the question. "Agent Hale, I believe I'm very close to uncovering some illegal activity but I'm not there yet. I think I may be able to find my answer this week."

She smirked. "You're obviously in a great deal of danger. You should consider breaching the attorney client privilege to protect yourself."

Sanders rubbed the irritated skin on his wrists. "I'm not willing to do that."

"Okay, Mr. Pierce. I just hope I don't end up seeing you in a body bag."

He sighed. "Me, too."

Agent Hale glanced down at her pad. "I assume you haven't told anyone at Global Data Systems that the FBI has contacted you about these information leaks."

Sanders nodded. "That's correct. I've told no one, not even Jackie Rogers, the General Counsel."

"Good."

"Agent Hale, can you tell me where the FBI is in its investigation?"

She shook her head. "No, I can't go into that."

He grimaced. "I understand. However, I beg you to give me one more week before you do anything major in the case. I'm afraid if the culprits get wind that the FBI is investigating, it will trigger a major cover up, making your job that much harder."

Agent Hale was laser-focused on Sanders. He remembered the exact look the first time he met her.

"You've got one week."

Chapter 23

An FBI agent dropped Sanders off at his townhouse. He felt hungry, sore, and tired.

Sanders called Beverly, Jackie's administrative assistant, and told her he was following up on a lead in the investigation and would not be coming into Global Data Systems until Thursday afternoon. He could not tell her he was kidnapped this morning.

After a hot shower and some lunch, he felt much better. His back still ached, and his wrists were tender from where the zip ties had irritated his flesh. Sanders opened his wallet and fished out the card Shay had given him to access the warehouse on Spangler Road.

Should I pay the warehouse a visit? He glanced at his watch. It was 3:30 p.m. *Although in the morning might be a better time.*

Sanders plopped down in his lounger with the Global Data Systems laptop. He checked his email inbox. Emma Peel had sent an email at 8:30 a.m. this morning.

Shay confirmed your connection. Warning: don't visit today. Thursday is a go, but not

Friday!
Emma

I dodged a bullet this time. Sanders rubbed his bald head. *If I hadn't been kidnapped, I would've gone to the warehouse today!*

He sent a reply.

I understand! Thank you.

Sanders picked up his phone, texted Claire, and asked if she would like to stop by at 5:00 p.m. for a glass of wine. She confirmed.

* * *

At 5:00 p.m., Sanders glimpsed out his study window and saw Claire walk by. He shot to his feet before she could ring his doorbell. Sanders swung open the door.

"You must be anxious to see me," she said with a smirk.

He smiled. "You have no idea what kind of day I've had."

"Well, invite me inside and you call tell me all about it."

They went up to the second floor living area. Sanders already had set two empty wine glasses on his kitchen counter.

"Ramey Chardonnay, okay?"

She nodded. "Perfect."

He poured two glasses of wine.

Claire walked over and plucked up his right hand. "What happen to your wrist?"

Sanders held up his other wrist as well. "I've a matching set."

Her eyes narrowed. "You didn't hurt yourself last night, did you?"

He shook his head. "No, let's go sit down and I'll fill you in on all the gory details."

They both settled into his Eames loungers.

"These wounds to my wrist are the result of having my hands zip-tied behind me. Some woman kidnapped me this morning."

Claire's mouth dropped open. "Are you serious?"

He nodded. "I'm afraid so. I was jogging early this morning over at UT Dallas. This woman came jogging towards me and doubled back around to get behind me. Before I knew it, she shot me with a taser gun."

"Oh my God, what happened then?"

Sanders took a sip of wine. "While I was incapacitated, she bound my wrists with zip ties. She then forced me into the trunk of her car. I spent the next half hour in there while she drove over to Oak Cliff. When she got out of the car and left to do something, I was able to kick the security trunk release lever and wiggle out of the trunk."

She patted his shoulder. "How did you know how to do that?"

He grimaced. "I learned it in a presentation at my old law firm. Since the early 2000s, every car must have such a lever. I saw a little button with a slight glow and assumed it was the lever."

"That's incredible, Sanders." Claire took a sip of wine. "What did you do after you escaped?"

"I grew up close to there and somewhat knew the area. It's a little strip section of stores and other buildings that use to be downtown Oak Cliff. It was still early enough in the morning so that none of the retail stores were open."

He took a sip of wine. "As I made my way down the street, I spotted the woman who kidnapped me coming out of a building, so I ducked in the alcove of a theatre. Fortunately, one of the doors was unlocked. The custodian there cut the zip ties off my wrists, and I called Agent Hale with the FBI."

"Isn't she—"

"She's the woman in the Lexus you saw dropping me off at my townhouse after we visited the campus where someone took a shot at me."

Her eyes widened. "What a crazy experience. You're lucky to be alive."

"I know!" He nodded and took a gulp of wine. "Do you remember the woman who approached our table at The Mansion bar?"

"Of course, the mysterious woman."

"Agent Hale thinks she's both the shooter and the kidnapper."

Claire set her empty wine glass down on the table

between them. "Sanders, this is getting scary. Are you close to finishing your assignment with Global Data Systems?"

Sanders drained his glass. "I believe I'm getting close to the end. I better be, because I'm tired of looking over my shoulder, wondering what's going to happen to me next."

"Can I get you another glass of wine? After the day you've had, you must need it."

He chuckled. "That would be nice. I'll just sit here and nurse my wounds."

Claire returned from the kitchen with two glasses of chardonnay. She arranged them on the table between them.

Sanders said, "Have you recovered from your encounter with that man last night?"

She squeezed her fist. "My hand is still a little sore, but otherwise I'm fine."

He picked up his glass of chardonnay and toasted her. "We make a fine pair with all our injuries, don't we?"

Claire laughed. "You're right. I've learned two lessons from last night. First, I'm not scheduling anymore night appointments. Second, I'm going to do a much more thorough job of screening before I agree to see anyone."

Sanders swirled the wine in his glass. "Since you're no longer booking late night appointments, then I guess I won't be getting anymore distress knocks on my bedroom wall from next door."

She smiled. "I might still knock, but not because I'm in danger."

He laughed. "Well, I still have a key to your front door. By the way, I have key to give you for my place. The way my life's going, I may be the one giving a distress knock on your wall."

She raised an eyebrow. "Seriously, Sanders, I've learned some lessons from my experience. What are you going to do to stay safe?"

Sanders sat up straight. "For starters, I'm staying away from that campus until this assignment is completed."

"Can't the FBI get more involved?"

He shook his head. "Not based upon the information I have given Agent Hale. Unless my client waives the attorney client privilege, I can't share any of what I've learned in my investigation. I've asked Agent Hale if the FBI was ramping up its investigation. She, of course, would not answer. To be honest, I want the FBI to hold off just a few more days so I can check out some more leads."

Claire frowned. "Sanders, I don't think that's a wise move. I wish you could tell me more about what's going on."

Sanders took a drink of wine. "I, too, wish I could tell you."

Chapter 24

Thursday, Sanders rolled out of bed at 7:00 a.m. This was the most restful night of sleep he had experienced in several days. His wrists were still a bit raw and his back ached, but he felt much better than yesterday.

Sanders chose a dark gray suit, white shirt and navy-blue tie. With a deep sigh, he gave up trying not to appear like a Global Data Systems employee.

Sanders was uncertain what his plan would be when he arrived at the warehouse later in the morning but surmised it might be helpful to blend in if necessary. He entered the parking lot at Spangler Road at 8:30 a.m., drove to the rear of the building, and pulled into a space alongside several other cars. Sanders sat in his Spider, staring at the door.

After a few minutes, he ambled up to the back door and ran the card Shay had given him through the card reader. The mechanism clicked as the lock unlocked. Sanders turned the knob and walk inside. His eyes darted right and left, surveying his surroundings.

He walked down a wide hallway. On each side were wood doors. Beside each door was another card reader.

Sanders approached the first door and slipped his card into the reader. It clicked like the front door of the building when the door unlocked. He nudged it open, wondering what was on the other side. It appeared to be a conference room containing a long-laminated table positioned in the middle of the room surrounded by several folding chairs. It had quite a spartan feel to it.

Whatever's going on here, they're not wasting money on expensive furniture.

A white board adorned one wall. Sanders studied the board. The word 'Targets' was written in red at the top of the board. Under Targets were four subheadings which read from left to right:

Sexual Transmittable Diseases, Mental Illness, AIDS, Miscellaneous. Underneath each subheading was a list of Names, Diseases, Treatments, Addresses, Occupations, Vulnerability Rating, and Status. The vulnerability ratings ranged from one to ten.

This health information must have been gleaned from the data in the second system. Sanders fished his phone out of his pocket and snapped several pictures of the board.

One thing's for certain, the second system is not used strictly for safekeeping purposes, if at all! He studied the board. *What does vulnerability mean?*

Sanders exited the room and proceeded down the hallway. A man's voice behind him called out, "Who are you?"

Sanders spun around. He stood face to face with

a large man with greased back black hair and a two-day old beard. From his light blue shirt and gray slacks, Sanders guessed the workers here were not subject to the same dress code enforced at Global Data Systems. The man's eyes scanned him from head to toe.

Sanders said, "I guess I could ask you the same question."

The man wrinkled his brow as his nose twitched.

Not expecting that question, were you? Sanders stifled a smirk.

"My name's Stuart Bonham. Now, who the hell are you?"

"Didn't Dan tell you I was stopping by?" He waited to see Stuart's reaction to his using the first name of the Beta Account Manager.

Stuart's eyes widened. "Do you mean Mr. Wooten?"

Sanders raised an eyebrow. "Of course, I mean Dan Wooten."

"I'm… sorry. No one… told me anyone was coming today. We have strict security here."

"What's your position here, Stuart?"

"I'm over the Batching Operators?"

Sanders glared at him. "If that's the case, I assume your group is first to receive the health data from Global Data Systems."

Stuart nodded. "Yes, that's correct."

"Care to give me a tour?"

Stuart wrinkled his forehead. "Do you have a security card?"

Sanders fished the card out of his coat pocket and gestured with it toward the conference room. "How do you think I got in here?"

Stuart squinted. "Only Dan and the two other Account Managers have security clearance to access that room."

Sanders walked over to the door to the conference room and slid the card through the reader. The door unlocked and he cracked it open. "Believe me now?"

Stuart's mouth dropped open. "Yes sir."

"Now would you care to please show me around?"

Stuart pointed down the hallway. "This way."

Sanders took a step back and motioned with his hand. "After you."

Stuart walked over to the next door down and slid his card through the reader. He held the door open for Sanders to enter first.

The physical layout of batching was identical to what he had seen at Global Data Systems. Eight operators sat in front of computers.

Stuart pointed in their direction. "My operators receive all the data from the Global Data System and then sort it by participant's name, disease diagnosis, treatment, dates of service and the employer health plan which covered the participant."

Sanders said, "What's the next step after the data is sorted?"

Stuart pointed toward the left wall. "The data is fed into Evaluation."

"What's the function of the Evaluation?"

Stuart shrugged. "I'm told it has to do with safekeeping."

Sanders raised an eyebrow. "What would be evaluated if the sole purpose is safekeeping?"

"You'll have to ask them."

"Who's over Evaluation?"

"Ted Giest manages the group."

Sanders motioned toward the door. "Will you introduce me?"

They walked into the hall and stood outside next-door. Stuart said, "I don't have security clearance here. My card won't work in that reader."

Sanders fished his card back out of his pocket and slid it through the card reader. The mechanism unlocked and Sanders pushed the door open. Six men were seated at computer terminals.

"Which one is Ted Giest?"

The man sitting at the nearest terminal said, "Ted's running an errand. He should be back soon."

Sanders approached him. "Dan asked me to familiarize myself with the operation here. Can you brief me on what you do in Evaluation?"

The man glanced over at Stuart. "Is it okay?"

Stuart said, "David, he has security clearance to open the door."

David looked up at Sanders. "I'm sorry. I just don't want to get in trouble."

Sanders patted him on the shoulder. "I understand but I'm in a bit of a hurry. So, if you could brief me on Evaluation, I'm sure Dan would approve."

Stuart said, "I'll leave you to it then." He exited the room.

David sighed. "We get all the sorted data from next door and then start a new sorting process."

Sanders cocked his head. "What are you sorting for a second time?"

David pointed at his computer screen. "Let me show you."

Sanders bent over so he could view his screen.

"This guy was diagnosed with bipolar depression. He's being treated by a psychiatrist. Here's a list of sessions he has seen the doctor. This is a list of the medications this doctor has prescribed for his treatment. The guy was specifically signaled out because he's a senior vice president in his company."

"Whoa, let me stop you there. How do you know a guy's position in the company from health records? That's not relevant to whether or not the company's health plan will cover a benefit."

The man nodded. "That's where the evaluation comes in. We feed all the information we sort into software that finds everything on the web about the targeted individual. The higher up in the company and the higher salary, the better."

Sanders eyes narrowed. "What happens next once you have all this information?"

The man waved a thumb over his shoulder. "Evaluations sends the sorted dated over to Investigations."

"I see. What exactly are they investigating?"

The man glanced over at the operators to make sure no one overheard. "The guys in Investigations are former private eyes. Then, I'm sure with your security clearance, you know what they're looking for."

The purpose of the second system was all coming crystal clear. "Of course."

Sanders glanced at his watch. He was concerned Ted Giest might return any minute and could be more suspicious than Stuart and David had been.

"Thank you for your time, David. I'll let Dan know how you stepped in and briefed me when the manager was out."

David smiled. "Thank you. Oh, by the way, I didn't get your name."

Sanders chuckled. "That's because I didn't tell you my name."

Sanders waved over his shoulder as he walked out of the room. He hurried down the hallway back to the front door. Sanders wanted to explore every room but had more than enough information about what went on in the confines of Suite 100, 10531 Spangler Road. He sat in the Spider, organizing his thoughts before driving away.

The three Global Data Systems health accounts send private health information offsite for one purpose and that's extortion. The data is sorted by disease, treatment, and the individual's status in the corporation. He tightened his grip on the steering wheel.

I suspect they determine their targets based upon

the potential embarrassment to the individual if the information was leaked to the wrong source and the individual's ability to pay to keep the information quiet. Sanders glanced in the rear view mirror. His face showed disgust.

The three Account Managers are clearly involved. I just wonder if it goes up higher than them!

As Sanders started up the Spider, a rotund bald man walked up to the entrance of the building. He surmised it might be Ted Giest returning from his errand.

How does he get away with wearing a light green shirt and khaki pants to work?

* * *

Sanders kept checking his rear view mirror to make sure he was not being followed. The enormity of what he just discovered sunk in. If he thought he was in danger before, it was now danger on steroids.

Am I one hundred percent certain? Is there any other reason for the operation at that warehouse to exist?

Sanders knew he needed to contact Agent Hale. His loyalty to Jackie Rogers outweighed that need. She should know first before he involved the FBI. He fished his phone out of his pocket and dialed Jackie, but it rolled to her administrative assistant, Beverly.

"Ms. Rogers office."

"Hi, Beverly, this is Sanders Pierce. Is Jackie

available to speak?"

"No, she's in a meeting until 5:00 p.m."

Sanders sighed. "This is especially important. Is there any way you could interrupt the meeting."

There was a pause at the other end of the line. "I don't think I could do that."

"Okay, is it possible for you to get her a message that I need to see her."

Beverly said in a clipped tone, "I'll see. What's your message?"

"Please tell her I've made a major breakthrough in my investigation. It's absolutely critical I speak with her this afternoon. The impact to Global Data Systems could be enormous."

"I'll get her the message. Where are you?"

Sanders glanced up at the overhead sign. "I'm on the North Dallas Tollway near the Beltline Road exit. I should be in my office in about fifteen minutes, depending upon traffic."

He checked his rear view mirror every few minutes to make sure no one was following him. Sanders felt a bit of relief when he passed by the security guard at the Global Data Systems gate. He found an empty space in Visitor Parking close to the entrance. Sanders stepped out of the Spider, grabbed his briefcase, and hurried up to the entrance of the building.

He passed through the usual maze of cubicles to his office. He unlocked his office door and closed it behind him.

Sanders plopped down in his office chair, grabbed a pen, and jotted notes on his legal pad. It was crucial he commit to writing everything he had witnessed at the Spangler Road warehouse.

He picked up his phone and pulled up the Photos App and studied the photos he had taken of the white board in the conference room. This exercise reaffirmed his conviction that his assessment was correct of the extortion scheme.

His phone buzzed on his desk. He scooped it up and answered. "Hi, Jackie."

"Sanders, what the hell is going on? I was in an important meeting with senior management."

He sighed. "I've discovered something that could be devastating for Global Data Systems. I need to meet with you in person."

After a pause, she said, "Okay, I'll need to get back to my meeting, but I'll get with you just as soon as possible."

"Thank you, Jackie."

Sanders leaned back in his chair and stared down at the surge protector. He wondered if his office was bugged again.

An hour later, Jackie knocked on his door, opened it, and scooted into his office, shutting it behind her. She slid into a client chair. "What's going on?"

He leaned forward. "Bottom line, I think I know the purpose of the second system out from Decryption."

Jackie wrinkled her forehead. "I recall you saying something about two systems, but could you refresh my memory?"

Sanders nodded. "Of course, the Beta, Delta, and Gamma Accounts have two systems that transfer decrypted data. One system goes internally to Batching and the second system carrying the identical data goes to a warehouse in northwest Dallas."

She straightened up in her chair. "That's right, you told me there was an offsite location."

He sighed. "Yes, I visited the site this morning."

Her eyes widened. "How did you discover it?"

"Do you remember me telling you about the Emma Peel emails?"

Jackie nodded. "Yes."

"She was able to corroborate what I learned in my interview. Not only that, but she put me in touch with a third person who told me the general location."

He paused. "Emma Peel, who really is Debra Brannon, the Quality Control Supervisor for the Gamma Account, is also the only Quality Control Supervisor who reports directly to an account manager. I assume they have something on her, because she's terrified. She felt compelled to help me but only via Emma Peel's cryptic emails. Do you follow me so far?"

Jackie nodded. "Yes, so far."

Sanders shifted in his chair. "I interviewed Lisa Hall, who is the administrative assistant to Dan Wooten. It's clear to me, Lisa does everything for Dan Wooten. She was able to confirm Dan signed a lease to rent a warehouse at 10531 Spangler Road in

Dallas. He told her he needed the warehouse to store some antique furniture."

Jackie pursed her lips. "I don't like where this is going."

"I went out to the warehouse on a recent weekend just to check it out. To gain entrance, you have to swipe a security card through a reader. So, I reached out to Debra, and she arranged for me to get one from the same third party as before."

Jackie narrowed her eyes. "Her sister, who's a stripper?"

Sanders smiled. "Yes, her younger sister."

She rolled her eyes. "Okay, go on with your story."

"Well, this morning, I headed over to the warehouse. I swiped the card and gained access to the building. Fortunately, I didn't initially encounter anyone. Each door inside had a card reader. I swiped my card in the first door I came across which opened into a conference room. There was a large white board at on one wall." He rattled off the subheadings and lists under the word 'Target'.

Sanders picked his phone up and accessed the Photo App. "These are pictures of the board."

Jackie squinted as she studied the screen. "What else did you discover?"

"When I exited the conference room, I was confronted by the manager over the operators that receive and sort the health information data from the Beta, Delta, and Gamma Accounts. I discovered by accident from him that my card had top security clearance because some cards are programmed to open only certain doors. That alone convinced this guy I had authority to be there. I did drop Dan Wooten's name several times to help the cause."

Jackie leaned back in her chair and stared at the ceiling. "So, this guy confirmed that the data received by the operators was definitely from Global Data Systems?"

Sanders nodded. "I'm afraid so. This guy said his group sorts the data received by each participant's name, disease diagnosis, treatment, dates of service, and the employer health plan which covered them. They send the sorted data over to an area called Evaluation."

"What happens there?"

"One of the operators in Evaluation told me this area sorts the data. Then they feed the individual's name into software to find out everything they can about his or her position in the company, salary, etc. The higher the better."

Jackie groaned. "I think I see now where this is headed."

Sanders twisted his mouth sideways. "Yes, that's about the time I was starting to understand myself. Anyway, the sorted data is sent to an area called Investigations. The operator in Evaluation told me the guys in that area are all ex-private investigators. At that point, I thought my luck might be running out, so I left without trying to get inside Investigations."

Jackie slapped the arms of her chair. "So, these

guys are running an extortion scheme, using the private health data of all our clients."

"Yes, it appears that's the case."

"You said Dan Wooten was one who leased the warehouse. Are you sure the other Account Managers are involved?"

Sanders leaned forward. "I think they would have to be involved. If not, they are grossly negligent in allowing a second system from their account to feed data to an offsite location. Besides, one of the guys I encountered said only the Account Managers have security to enter the conference room. Also, I learned through my interviews that the three of them meet offsite on a regular basis. I suspect the meeting takes place in the conference room at the warehouse."

Jackie stood up and paced back and forth. "When this information gets out to the public, it will destroy our whole health claims processing line of business."

"Jackie, I wouldn't be surprised if it destroyed all of Global Data Systems, when you factor in client mistrust across the board and all the lawsuits that will occur."

She slumped into her chair. "You're probably right. I'm going to have to contact the FBI about this matter."

Sanders glanced down at his legal pad. "There's only one other uncertainty I would like to investigate."

Jackie narrowed her eyes. "You're wondering how high up the food chain this goes, aren't you?"

He nodded. "Shall we start at the top?"

"I'll get us on Dick White's calendar tomorrow."

After Jackie left his office, Sanders pulled up the organization chart for Global Data Systems. The Beta, Delta, and Gamma Account Managers reported directly to Vice President, David Simms. He reports directly to Dick White, the President.

Sanders leaned back in his chair and closed his eyes. *I hate to do this without telling Jackie, but I need to call Agent Hale!*

He picked up his phone up off the desk and dialed her number.

Agent Hale answered on the second ring. "Agent Hale."

"Agent, this is Sanders Pierce."

"How can I help you, Mr. Pierce."

He sighed. "I have some information that would be of interest to you which clearly falls outside of the attorney client privilege. I think it might be better if we met in person if possible."

"I agree, Mr. Pierce. Can you come here, or would you like me to meet you somewhere?"

"Yes, I can come there. When would you like to meet?"

"Time is of the essence. Can you come now?"

Sanders checked his watch. It was 3:00 p.m.

He had forgotten about eating lunch. With the pit in his stomach, he had no appetite. He did not care about the fate of Global Data Systems. But he knew his investigation had the potential to lead to a lot of employees losing their jobs, including Jackie Rogers.

Sanders arrived at the Dallas FBI headquarters at 3:45 p.m. A young woman ushered him up to a meeting room on the third floor.

Agent Hale walked into the room and shut the door behind her. She plopped down in the chair across from Sanders and set her bag on the table next to her. He watched as she pulled a pad of paper and pen out of her bag and arranged them in front of her.

After Agent Hale was settled in, she glanced up at him. "Mr. Pierce, I assume since you're here, you have discovered something illegal in your investigation."

Sanders nodded. "Yes, I believe that Global Data System's clients' private health information is being used for extortion purposes."

Her eyes were laser focused on Sanders. "How did you make this discovery?"

"Let me give you some background for context. During the interviews I conducted with various employees in the Beta, Delta, and Gamma, I learned about a second system used to transfer health data. As I'm sure you know, federal law requires claims administrators to encrypt private health data until it is decrypted for purposes of adjudicating the health claims on the health plan participants."

Agent Hale jotted on her pad. Without looking up, she said, "Yes, I'm aware of that legal requirement."

Sander leaned forward. "In all three accounts, after the data is decrypted, one system properly sends the data to the Batching Department to be assigned to whichever employer's health plan provides coverage, so the adjudication process can begin. A second system sends the identical data to an offsite location in Dallas."

She stopped writing and glanced up. "How did you learn about this offsite location?"

"Again, through interviews and the help of a woman who had inside knowledge. Apparently, this woman took a huge risk in assisting me. I'm not certain what the account managers have on her, but she's scared of something. She communicated with me through cryptic emails and identified herself as Emma Peel. Although you're younger than I am, I'm sure you've heard of Emma Peel."

Agent Hale nodded. "Of course, please continue."

"She also tipped me that my office was bugged. I had an outside company do a sweep and indeed a bug was found in the surge protector under my desk. Also my email had been manipulated so someone could access it."

Agent Hale tapped her pen on the pad. "Do you know the identity of this person other than as Emma Peel?"

Sanders nodded. "Yes, her name's Debra Brannon. She's a Quality Control Manager for the Gamma Account and the only Quality Control Manager who reports directly to the Account Manager. Anyway, Ms. Brannon, through her cover as Emma Peel, put me touch with a person outside of Global Data Systems. This person gave me the general location of where the second system was sending the data.

Emma Peel also managed to get me a security card to access the card reader at the offsite location."

Agent Hale looked up from her notes. "Do you have the address?"

He nodded. "Yes, it's a warehouse at 10531 Spangler Road, Suite 100, in northwest Dallas."

She jotted in her pad. "Did you ever get inside this warehouse?"

Sanders pulled his phone out of his coat pocket. "Yes, I visited the warehouse this morning." He handed his phone to Agent Hale. "These are pictures I took of the white board in one of the rooms."

She studied the photographs. "Very interesting. What else did you find in this warehouse?"

"I was able to convince one of the managers I was part of the scheme, based solely on my security card. The card readers are programmed so only the highest security clearance can open any door." He fished his security card out of his coat pocket and held it out to Agent Hale. "This card will open any door in the building."

She examined the card, removed an envelope from her bag, and slipped the card inside. "What else did you find?"

"This manager was over the operators who retrieved the health information data from Global Data Systems. These operators sort the data by participant's name, diseases, diagnosis, dates of service, and the employer health plan which covered the participant."

Agent Hale jotted on her pad. "Did this manager confirm that the data was received from Global Data Systems."

Sanders nodded. "Yes, I specifically asked him that question and he answered in the affirmative."

"What happens to this sorted data?"

"It's sent next to an area called Evaluation. At this stage, this group sorts the data by name of the participant, certain diagnoses such as bi-polar depression and treatment. They then feed the data into some software which brings up everything on the web about this individual, salary, position in the company, etc. This sorted data is sent to area called 'Investigations'. The guy in Evaluations told me that Investigations is composed of ex-private investigators. I was worried my luck might luck run out, so I decided I had enough information to know crimes were being committed."

Agent Hale pursed her lips. "These guys in Investigations probably identify certain individuals to target for extortion."

"My conclusion as well."

She set her pen down. "I've got all I need for probable cause that crimes have been committed."

He leaned back in his chair. "The only thing I don't know is how high up the corporate ladder knowledge of this extortion scheme goes. The General Counsel is trying to get us a meeting with the President tomorrow."

Agent Hale narrowed her eyes. "You've shared

this information about the warehouse with her?"

Sanders nodded. "Yes, I told her earlier today."

"Did it ever occur to you she might be involved in this scheme as well?"

He straightened up in his chair. "I've known Jackie a long time. There's no way she would be involved in anything illegal."

Agent Hale closed her pad and slipped it into her bag. "Would you send me those photographs you took of the white board?"

He picked up his phone and accessed the app. "Done. Agent Hale, I know you won't disclose the FBI's next steps in this matter, but if you will give me until close of business tomorrow, I might have the answer as to everyone who's involved in this scheme."

She dropped her phone in the bag. "I'll take that under advisement."

"Thank you."

Agent Hale leaned in. "I assume you realize you're in grave danger until we escalate our investigation."

Sanders grimaced. "Yes, I'm acutely aware of that."

As Sanders drove home from his meeting with Agent Hale, he ran the day's events through his head.

Did I miss anything?

He thought about his next appearance at the office. *I'm both dreading and curious about meeting with the President of Global Data Systems. What will be his reaction?*

Sanders turned right on Preston Road onto

Campbell. A white sedan behind him had made every turn since he exited the North Dallas Tollway. The driver kept a safe distance.

As Sanders proceeded east on Campbell, he watched to see if the car still followed him. He stopped at a red light at the intersection of Coit Road and Campbell Road. The white sedan was now right behind him. The driver of the white car was a man in sunglasses, staring straight at the rear of the Spider.

If he takes a left on Mimosa, then there's little doubt he's following me.

Mimosa Drive dead-ended into his community, Lake Park Estates. Sanders took a left on Mimosa and so did the white car. His heart raced as he hit the button on his fob to open the front gate to the community.

Sanders sped inside and the car entered as well, staying within a few feet of his bumper. He took a left and then an immediate right on to his street, Grove Park Lane. The white car took the same left and right but slowed down and paralleled park several yards south of Sanders' townhouse.

After pulling into his garage, Sanders lowered the garage door. He exhaled and concluded the guy was perhaps one of his neighbors.

Chapter 25

Friday morning, Sanders arrived at his office at 8:00 a.m. on the dot. After he was settled, he opened his email. The previous evening at 8:30 p.m. Jackie had sent an email.

> Sanders, we have a meeting with Dick White at 9:30 a.m. I am booked until then so I will meet you in his office. It is on the fifteenth floor. The receptionist is right outside the elevators. She will escort you to Dick's office. Jackie

Sanders had hoped he could discuss strategy with Jackie before the meeting but that obviously was not in the cards. He arrived on the fifteenth floor at 9:15 a.m. The receptionist informed him Dick White would be available in a few minutes and suggested he have a seat in a small lounge area nearby.

As Sanders took in his surroundings, he noticed how luxurious the carpet was, compared to the lobby on the first floor. The furniture was top of the line contemporary.

He took a seat in what he guessed was a B.&B. Italia chair. At 9:45 a.m., the receptionist escorted him over to an elaborate wood door and knocked.

Jackie opened the door. She had dark bags under her eyes and was as pale as a ghost. Sanders assumed she had not slept much the prior night.

Jackie gestured toward the left leather client chair which sat at the foot of a huge walnut desk. "Have a seat, Sanders."

A stocky man, with thinning white hair dressed in the usual corporate charcoal gray suit, white shirt, and navy-blue tie sat behind the desk. He wore a frown and was staring at Sanders. Sanders slid into the seat and Jackie sat in the seat next to him.

She said, "Dick, this is Sanders Pierce. As you know, he was retained to help with the investigation of the health information leaks."

"Jackie tells me," Dick said, "you've made quite a discovery."

Sanders eyes widened. Jackie had gone ahead and discussed the matter without him.

Sander sat up straight. "Yes, we've found the source of the leaks."

Clenching his jaw, Dick said, "Tell me about these findings."

"Well, there's a second system in all three Health Accounts that transfers data to an offsite location in Dallas. Through my interviews and investigation, I was able to learn the location of this offsite."

Dick said, "Stop, right there. Who told you the location?"

Sanders pondered how to answer. He was not

inclined to reveal the identity of Emma Peel yet. Sanders was uncertain of what Jackie had already discussed with Dick.

He shifted in his chair. "An individual with this knowledge who wanted to remain anonymous provided me encrypted tips which led to the discovery of the location."

Jackie said, "This anonymous person is the Manager of Quality Control for the Gamma Account."

Sanders' eyebrows shot up. *How could Jackie blurt out the identity of my source?*

Dick groaned. "Go on, Pierce."

"I was able to get a security card to access the building located on Spangler Road in northwest Dallas."

Dick pounded his desk with his right fist. "How the hell did you get a security card?"

Jackie said, "From the same person who informed him of the location."

Sanders felt a pit in his stomach. *What's going on here?*

Dick glared at him. "I assume you visited this building."

Sanders nodded. "Yes, I did yesterday morning. I got to see enough of this operation to know Global Data client health information is being illegally used for what can only be extortion purposes."

Dick muttered through a clenched jaw, "He knows everything."

Jackie said, "Yes, I told you."

Sanders glanced over at her, but she was staring straight ahead.

Dick pressed a button on his intercom. "Send in Ms. Dark."

A side door to his office slid opened and a tall, athletic woman wearing all black entered the room. Sanders recognized her as the woman who had kidnapped him.

Dick said, "I believe you've already become acquainted with Ms. Dark."

Sanders sank in his chair. "Unfortunately, I'm acquainted with her."

Dick said, "Ms. Dark, please take our guest to the boiler room and dispose of him."

Ms. Dark pulled a pistol out of a holster concealed under her jacket. "Let's go. You won't be doing your Houdini act a second time."

A chill shot down Sanders' spine. He was shaking but managed to get to his feet. He glanced back at Jackie. "Why did you hire me? Why are you doing this?"

She sighed. "I'm sorry, Sanders. I thought you would be perfect for this investigation. I just didn't think you would be successful. If I wanted the investigation to be successful, I could have hired over a dozen attorneys that are intimately more qualified than a retired attorney-turned-artist."

Ms. Dark shoved him toward the side door. She opened it and pushed him through it. They entered a small room with a solitary elevator.

She pushed the button and the doors to the elevator slid open without making much of a sound. "Get in."

She followed him inside, hit a button marked with a letter "B", and shoved the pistol into his ribs. The elevator jolted a bit as it descended.

Sanders' eyes darted around, trying to devise some plan of action. After what seemed like several minutes, the elevator opened in the basement of Global Data Systems.

Ms. Dark poked him with the pistol. "Get out."

Sanders stumbled out of the elevator, and she followed right behind him a few steps.

A woman's voice shouted, "Freeze, FBI."

Both Ms. Dark and Sanders spun around. Two men with dark suits and Agent Hale had their pistols drawn and aimed at Ms. Dark.

Agent Hale said, "Drop the pistol and put your hands up!"

Ms. Dark froze, as if trying to decide whether to obey the command or shoot her way out. After a few more seconds, she dropped the pistol and it clanked on the concrete floor. One of the agents kicked the gun a few yards away while the other agent handcuffed her.

Agent Hale said, "Are you all right, Mr. Pierce?"

Sanders exhaled. "I'm okay. But, how did you know I was here?"

"Jackie Rogers contacted us last night and informed us of your meeting this morning. When she told Dick White yesterday the purpose of why you wanted meet with him, he panicked and offered her two million dollars to help with a cover-up. This jerk thought he had persuaded her to accept the money. She wore a wire and played along so we could get it all on the record."

Sanders rubbed his forehead. "Thank God. She played her part so well that I was even convinced she was involved."

Agent Hale patted him on the shoulder. "I'm glad she was such a good actor. Otherwise, this could have ended rather badly for you."

Sanders watched as the agents placed Ms. Dark in the back of a car. *I'd prefer to see them put her in the trunk.*

Sanders entered the lobby of Global Data Systems and made his way through the maze of cubicles one last time to his office. He felt a profound sadness for all the innocent employees who would without a doubt lose their job because of the corruption of a few individuals high up in the corporate ranks.

Sanders plopped down in his chair and stared at his legal pad. *I never dreamt this would be the result of my investigation.*

After a few moments, he picked up his phone and dialed Claire's number.

She answered right away. "Hey, Sanders, what's up?"

"I'm going to purchase the most expensive bottle of wine I can find on my way home this evening and

I need someone to share it with. Are you available?"

"Absolutely. What should I wear for this special occasion?"

"Anything but a dark gray suit and white shirt. Be comfortable."

"That sounds promising." She paused. "Hey, is everything all right?"

"You won't believe what I'm going to tell you."

They hung up.

A knock came at his door and he looked up. Jackie stood in the doorway. Sanders met her in the middle of his office, and they hugged.

She said, "Are you okay?"

"I'm fine, but how are you?"

"Retired."

Sanders laughed. "I don't blame you. Not much of a future here."

Jackie slid into one of the client chairs and Sanders into the other one.

She said, "What an experience."

He nodded. "I was just thinking... I never imagined this would be the outcome."

Jackie sighed. "Yep. I agree."

Sanders scratched his head. "Why would the president of a company as successful as Global Data Systems risk so much for a few extra dollars gotten through extortion?"

She groaned. "Pure greed!"

"That's sad. However, I do have one question though, Jackie."

"What's that?"

He smiled. "Did you really have several attorneys lined up for this job who were more qualified than I am?"

She laughed. "Let's just say you were my first choice."

Acknowledgments

This is my fourth novel in this series. Treaty Oak Publishers via Cynthia Stone has provided stellar guidance in all aspects from editing to suggesting cover ideas on each of the novels. I am truly grateful to her for all the talents she has lent to my novels.

I am also thankful for Kim McBride for her design work in bringing the cover to life.

ABOUT THE AUTHOR

Jim Lively is currently the Artist and Curator at Martsolf Lively Contemporary in Richardson, Texas. After practicing law for many years, Jim decided to pursue his passion full time as a visual artist, film maker, and author. He received the 2016 Merrimack Media Outstanding Writer Award for his second novel, **Punitive Damages. *Choking on the Splinters*** is the third novel in a series, a Global Book Bronze Award winner for Mystery and Suspense. **Surreal Absurdity**, also a Global Book Bronze Award winner, is a sequel to his novel, **Aberrant Behavior**.

His artwork and art films have been recognized in numerous juried competitions, publications and film festivals. He has exhibited his artwork in several group and solo exhibitions across North America and Europe.

Fourteen of Jim's films have been selected to various film festivals around the world. His art film, **The Soul of Vinyl, Abbey Road Side 2**, screened at the 2016 New York City Independent Film Festival. Jim's film, **The Case of the Deranged**

Sommelier, won Best Experimental Film in the 2016 Directors Circle of Shorts Film Festival and the 2017 Lion's Head Film Festival. His film, *Still Mad as Hell*, screened at the 2017 New York City Independent Film Festival. His latest film, *It's Gonna Disappear*, screened at the 2021 New York Flash Film Festival.

Jim's education includes a Bachelor of Arts from The University of Texas at Austin, a Juris Doctor from Southern Methodist University in Dallas, and Level One Wine Sommelier Certification from the International Wine and Spirits Guild.

www.ingramcontent.com/pod-product-compliance
Lightning Source LLC
Chambersburg PA
CBHW071602180626
46819CB00002B/103